BOOK THREE

QUARANTINE

theBURNOUTS

LEX THOMAS

QUARANTINE

theBURNOUTS

BOOK THREE

Carolrhoda LAB

MINNEAPOLIS

First published by Egmont USA in 2014

Copyright © 2014 by Lex Thomas

Carolrhoda Lab™ is a trademark of Lerner Publishing Group, Inc.

Carolrhoda Lab™
An imprint of Carolrhoda Books
A division of Lerner Publishing Group, Inc.
241 First Avenue North
Minneapolis, MN 55401 USA

For reading levels and more information, look up this title at
www.lernerbooks.com.

Library of Congress Cataloging-in-Publication Data

Thomas, Lex.
    The Burnouts / Lex Thomas.
       pages cm. — (Quarantine ; book three)
    In this final installment of the Quarantine trilogy, David and Will are alive, but on the outside of McKinley High, while Lucy is the last of the trinity left inside to deal with Hilary, who will exact revenge before taking over McKinley High.
     ISBN 978-1-60684-338-3 (hardcover) — ISBN 978-1-5124-0115-8 (EB pdf)
     [1. Quarantine—Fiction. 2. Survival—Fiction. 3. High schools—Fiction.
4. Schools—Fiction. 5. Science fiction.] I. Title.
PZ7.T366998Bu 2014
[Fic]—dc23   2014003027

Manufactured in the United States of America
2 — SB — 12/31/15

To Robocop.

Thanks for keeping the city safe.

1

"I THOUGHT YOU WERE DEAD," WILL SAID.

"I'm sorry," David said. "I can't imagine what that was like for you."

David wore a gas mask. His breath was loud through its filters. He breathed slow and steady, like an iron lung. The mask wasn't like the ones that Will had seen the military wear. Twin black cylindrical air filters hung off the chin, and a clear plastic face shield allowed Will to see all of David's face from his lower lip up. His eye was smiling. There had been so many things Will had regretted not saying to David when he'd found out he was dead, and now he was at a loss for words.

Will looked around the overdecorated Airstream trailer. It hadn't been the worst place to count down the hours until he was virus-free. The place had a bed, a kitchenette, an eating nook with seating for two, and a couch. Orange light from amber bulbs in thrift-store lamps warmed the room. Floral design contact paper covered the countertop. Plaid curtains over tiny windows looked out to black night. The trailer had definitely been decorated by one of the mothers, by a chorus of mothers, maybe. There were comforting touches everywhere. Ruffles hanging off things, embroidered pillows, fanciful books aimed at middle schoolers. Newsprint hangman and Mad Libs activity booklets like you see in truck stops. There were teddy bears. Four bears to be exact—a black one, a polar bear, a koala, and a hot-pink one that was half the size of the others. He'd found them arranged in a line at the head of the bed. The fridge was plastered with Disney cartoon refrigerator magnets. There were decorative wooden signs hanging, with words like *Love* and cheerful phrases like *Tomorrow is a new day.*

"Who told you I was dead?" David said.

"One of the kids from the outside, the Saints, he said he saw a body with a white eye patch in a house that sounded like ours. I didn't know what else to think."

David sagged and shook his head. "I never imagined that you'd hear about that."

"Hear about what?" Will said. "I don't understand."

David started to say something and then stopped. His good eye wandered toward the kitchenette window. Will's stomach started to knot.

"Ugh, so dramatic." Will said. "You're killing me over here."

David laughed. Will had forgotten what that sounded like. It was a good sound.

"When I got out, it wasn't what I'd expected. There was no one in town. Not even the military. I limped through downtown, and every store was empty, every house deserted. I felt like I'd never see another human being, but then I did."

David swatted away a fly that had landed on his face shield.

"Two guys in haz-mat suits in a red pickup truck. They saw my white hair and must have assumed I was still infected, 'cause they fired on me. I ran, but they started hunting me through town. I barely got away from them, and when I did, I headed straight home."

"To our house?" Will said with wonder. He'd spent countless nights in McKinley thinking of their family home. Sometimes, imagining he was there, in his room, had been the only way he could get to sleep. "Is it the same?"

David winced. "Dad was out of town when the infection hit, so our house didn't get boarded up like the others. The windows were all shattered. The front door was hanging off its hinges. I went in and the living room looked like a drained pond. Junk on the floor, black mold all over the carpet. Animals had shit on the coffee table. The old couch was torn to pieces."

Each detail stung Will anew. He and David and their parents had played Pictionary and eaten pizza on that couch more times than he could remember.

"I found that old family photo on the mantel. Remember the one that Mom made us all wear Charlie Brown sweaters in?"

Will had always hated that photo. He looked like an idiot in it, but it had always made his mother laugh. Hearing about it now, he longed to see it again. He was starting to forget what her face looked like.

"Do you still have it?" Will asked.

"I wish. I was sitting in the easy chair by the big bay window—"

"The comfy chair?"

David smiled. "Yeah, the comfy chair. I was sitting there, staring at the picture, when this kid comes stomping down the stairs. White hair—infected."

"He was living in our house?!" Will said, outraged.

"Oh, yeah, he'd set up shop, all right. He was wearing four sets of my clothes and waving around Mom's butcher knife."

"And you didn't have a mask or anything?"

David shook his head, dead serious. "I held my breath."

"Jesus."

"He started shouting, 'Yo, this is MY spot! Who the hell are you?' Then he stopped right in front of the bay window. He looks at me sideways, lowers the knife to his side, and goes, 'I know you. . . . You're in all the pictures.' Then the window exploded. Out of nowhere. Machine guns blasting, and the kid got drilled with bullets. Dropped dead."

"Holy shit."

"I peeked out the window, fucking terrified, and I see the red pickup truck and those two hunters again, heading for the front door. My lungs were burning, I thought for sure I was going to die if didn't run for it, but I also knew that they'd tracked me to our house. If they saw that they'd killed someone else, they'd keep on hunting me. That's when I got the idea. The dead kid was about my size . . . so I grabbed a shard of glass and shoved it in his eye, then slipped my eye patch over it. I felt like my lungs were gonna pop. I jumped out the window and booked it out of there."

David sat back as the story settled over Will.

"Whoa." It was all Will could manage to say.

"I was just trying to throw the hunters off my trail. I never wanted you to hear about it. I had no idea."

"It's okay," Will said. "I think I'll get over it."

He was downplaying it for a laugh, but the truth was, having his brother back felt like a miracle.

"I missed you," Will blurted out, and then felt awkward.

"Missed you too, shithead."

Will laughed. But then there was that uncomfortable silence again. The walkie-talkie on David's hip squelched and he turned it down.

"How long have you been working with the parents?" Will said.

"A while."

Will almost didn't ask, but he needed to know. "Were

you with them when they trapped us back inside?"

David shook his head. "But . . . I can understand why they did it."

Will couldn't hide his shock. "Really? How can you possibly say that?"

"Nothing's like it used to be, Will," David said. "The whole country's . . . sick. They're not afraid to murder infected teens—laws or no laws. These parents here, all they want to do is protect their sons and daughters from the maniacs out there."

"What about the maniacs inside school?"

"Like the ones that pull kids' heads off in front of their dads?"

Will sank in his seat. He felt his cheeks warm.

"I told you it was an accident," Will said. "I never would have done that on purpose, believe me. But the guy gave me no other choice! He said I couldn't leave without Sam. Sam was already dead, so I did what I had to do."

David's face didn't offer the forgiveness he'd hoped for. "I'm not gonna lie . . . it's a problem. Sam's dad pretty much runs the farm. And he doesn't like you, to say the least."

"Do they make 'sorry I pulled off your son's head' greeting cards?"

David stared at Will blankly. Will felt a pinch of dread. Maybe the joke was in bad taste, but come on, this was Sam they were talking about. David burst out laughing. It made

Will trust him again, really for the first time since he'd discovered he was alive. Will smiled. If David was still the guy who hated Sam, then he was still his brother.

"Don't worry," David said. "Whatever happens, we'll figure it out."

That warmed Will. David would always have his back.

"Well, I guess we should get to it," David said.

"Get to what?"

David picked a toolbox off the floor. He put it on the table. He opened it and pulled out a small plastic box full of needles, alcohol towelette packets, and thin strips of red paper.

"Lemme see your hand," David said.

Will produced it. David took hold of his index finger and stabbed it with a lancet.

"Ow! What the fuck?" Will said, and yanked his hand back. A bead of blood swelled on his fingertip.

"Quit being a baby," David said with a little smile. He took Will's hand again, picked up one of the red strips of paper from his toolbox, and touched it to the blood bead. The blood spread eagerly through the pores of the paper. David held the strip up to the thrift-store lamp behind him. Will waited for a reaction.

"Is it supposed to do something?"

"If you were still infected, the blood would dissolve the paper. And . . . that's not happening," David said. "Congratulations, you're officially virus-free."

He pulled off his mask. The sight of David's whole face, unobscured by a breathing device, made Will tear up. For the first time since Will and the Loners had lugged David to the ruins, bruised as an old pear, there were no barriers between them. No fence. No mask. No virus. David breathed the same air as Will. Somehow, David's new black eye patch and dark hair made him look more intimidating than the white one ever did. He looked more grown up. He was six inches taller than Will, with broader shoulders. David would always be bigger than him, because graduating early meant Will had finished puberty early. He'd be this size forever.

Will gave his eyes a quick rub so David wouldn't see they were wet.

"You're just as ugly as I remember," Will said.

"Did you get shorter?" David volleyed back.

"Good to know you're still not funny."

"Rather be unfunny than have breath like yours. Do you eat diapers?" David said, waving his hand in front of his nose.

Will chuckled, and felt better, but his smile soon faded. There was something else he wanted to ask.

"Is Dad out there?"

David blinked a lot but his mouth remained still.

"I never got out of the infected zone. Once I got word the parents were here, I made my way back. I figured maybe Dad would be here."

"Was he?" Will said. He felt a rush of hope.

"No. But I'm sure he's alive. Somewhere. We'll find him eventually."

"Sure," Will said, already reburying that hope, deep, back where it belonged.

Will searched for another joke to fill the silence but came up empty.

"Everything's going to be okay now, Will. We're together. I think the bad part is over."

It had been longer than he could remember since anyone had told him that things would be okay, and he hadn't known how much he needed to hear it. Will lost his battle to keep from crying. Tears blurred the world, and spilled from his eyes, but David didn't notice. He walked over to the window in the door of the trailer and he peered through the glass, because people had started screaming outside.

David threw open the door to the night outside. A strange orange light flooded in and made David into a silhouette.

"Come on! We have to help," David said as he bounded out the door.

The farm was ablaze.

2

THERE WERE CHICKENS ON FIRE. LITTLE TUFTS
of flame screaming and squawking for mercy. They raced
around on the dark lawn, weaving between each other, until
they flopped over and died. Beyond the smoldering chickens
was a blazing structure. Flames licked the night from its roof,
and a crowd of parents was gathered around it, trying to put
out the fire. They hucked buckets of water at it. Shoveled dirt.
The fire only grew.

It was hot. The air stuck to Will. It made his clothes heavy.

"Distraction . . . ," David muttered from beside Will. Then
he yelled at the crowd, "It's a distraction! We're under attack!"

No one by the fire turned. They didn't hear. Will looked
where David was looking, easily three hundred yards from
the fire, to a section of the two-story wall of stacked tractor
trailers that surrounded the farm. There were people there,
dropping down from a ladder leaned against the wall. Will

could see maybe three or four of them in the full moonlight, but his eyes were still adjusting.

"Come on," David said, and tugged Will away from the fence that encircled the Airstream.

Will followed David's lead as they sprinted in a zigzag through a waist-high crop of tomatoes. David's agility surprised Will, considering his brother was blind in one eye. The last time he'd seen David run, the guy had been as steady as an unmanned bicycle. David leapt over a row of plants and kept running.

They were getting closer to the people who had dropped down from the wall. There were five of them now, running across a lumpy, tilled lawn toward the school. Bearded men with beer bellies that shook when they ran. One, with a dark mesh baseball cap, pointed in Will's direction and threw something at the brothers.

Will heard a *plunk* in the dirt nearby.

"Move!" David yelled. David bounded away, yanking Will by the shirt. A cracking *boom* blasted them off their feet. He landed facedown in a pile of cold earth. Dirt and stems and burned leaves rained down on him. David pulled him up.

"You okay?"

"Yeah," Will said, even though he wasn't.

David swallowed. "They've got grenades."

Will thought, *He must be joking.*

The bearded men pulled grenades out of the hefty duffel

bags they carried and hurled them at the school. The parents handling the fire heard the blasts that followed, and they went into a panic, grabbing weapons and scurrying around. The night lit up with explosions. Dirt sprayed into the air. Cows burst into pieces.

"This way!" David shouted.

Will ran after David to the ladder against the farm wall. His brother was already halfway up it. It jolted and clanged with every rung David climbed. Will followed. The thunderclap of an explosion behind Will made him jerk and freeze up.

"Don't stop," David said from above. "You're okay."

Will looked up to see his brother standing on the ledge of the wall, reaching down for him. The moon encircled David's head like it was an emblem. Will continued up. At the top David grabbed him by the arm and helped him the rest of the way. As Will rose up, his view expanded past the wall.

Will stopped breathing. Pale Ridge spread out in front of him. The world he remembered, the town where he'd lived for his entire life, was right there beneath the shimmering white-caps of the Rockies. Home. He'd been born in Sisters of Mercy Hospital right in the middle of town and had lived his whole life at 335 Butterfield Lane, playing in Mint Creek, walking to Frontier Elementary. His whole life whooshed through his brain, and it felt real, instead of a pale, distant memory.

David grabbed his arm. "Will, what are you doing?"

"Sorry." Will shook it off and faced his brother.

David stood next to a folding lawn chair with a pickax leaning against it. He snatched up the pickax and handed it to Will. Grenades blasted behind them.

"There's more people coming. I need you to keep them off the wall. Can you do that?"

"I . . . guess."

"Not 'you guess.' Yes."

"Yes. I got it. But who are these guys?"

"Hunters," David said. "Watch the wall." He turned away but stopped. "And, Will—" He locked onto Will with his one serious eye. "Don't die, okay? I just got you back."

Never in his life had David spoken to him with this much trust. The David he remembered never would have let him from his sight. He would have told him to run and hide while he took care of things. Not now.

"I'll be okay. What are you gonna do?"

"I'm gonna help put out that fire," David said, and he took off down the length of the wall, toward the blazing building.

Another explosion rocked the night. Then a cluster of them like a fireworks finale. Will looked down at the farm. The tractor-trailer barrier ran like the Great Wall of China around a patchwork of crops, outbuildings, and smaller fenced-in areas, hugging them close to the school, which for the first time didn't seem titanic to Will.

A flash of light burst out from a third-floor ledge after a grenade didn't reach the roof. The hunters had reached the school. On the next throw, they might get it right, and the parents defending the school were in high gear to stop it.

Three parents on the school's roof dared to rise over the ledge with rifles and fired down at the hunters. They missed. The hunters were working their way toward the industrial elevator that provided roof access. A parent in work overalls and an orange bandanna headband sent a hatchet flying at the hunters. It sunk into the hip of the hunter in the dark baseball cap and the man shrieked. Another hunter raised up a grenade to throw at the parents, but an arrow cut through the dark and planted itself in his thigh. He fell to the ground with his gym bag. The live grenade tumbled into the dark dirt nearby. Everyone scattered.

A blast of white fire. The bags of grenades detonated. The resulting blast lit up the whole school and forced Will to close his eyes to keep from being blinded. His ears rang. Nothing remained of the two hunters. Will looked to the roofline where two of the parents cheered while the third, a tubby one with a compound bow, stared at the carnage he'd sparked.

A clang sounded off behind Will, on the outer farm wall. Then, the aluminum rattle of a ladder. Two more hunters were climbing up a ladder twenty feet from Will, onto the wall. They had guns strapped to their backs.

Will tightened up on his pickax and ran at them. The pounding of his feet on the hollow metal trailers was like church bells, alerting the hunters to climb faster. As the highest hunter reached the top of the ladder, Will swung his pickax at him.

"Yagh!" The hunter slid down a few rungs.

"Stay off!" Will said.

The hunter reached to his back with one hand, where his rifle was. Will dropped the pickax and grabbed the ladder with both hands. Will strained, drawing on all the strength in his thighs and arms. The ladder lifted away from the wall. The second hunter cut his losses and scrambled down to the ground. The first hunter leveled his rifle at Will.

David wouldn't be coming to save him. This was on him. If he died, there was a chance the school would be sacked and the kids inside murdered. In a flash he understood why the parents had been doing things the way they'd been doing them.

Will shoved the ladder away from the wall, and the hunter's gun fired up into the air.

The ladder dropped, screeching the whole way down. Will turned toward the school, heaving breath. He saw that the parents had finally gained the advantage. All of the hunters were fleeing toward the gate out of the farm. All but one.

"You're gonna die, rat lover," a voice said from below Will.

"I'll take you with me, prick," another voice said.

Will crept to the farm-side ladder with his pickax. A stocky hunter with a bowie knife shuffled toward a silver-haired parent with an athletic build. The parent was on the ground, clutching his ankle. His only weapon was a motorcycle helmet. Black.

Sam's dad.

Will was fast onto the ladder. At the bottom in seconds. The hunter lunged at Sam's dad with the bowie knife, but he got a pickax through his own shoulder instead. The hunter screamed and fell to the ground beside Sam's father.

Will approached the hunter. The man was squirming in the dirt and trying to reach back to the pickax. He looked over to Sam's dad, who was studying him with a skeptical face. A stream of profanity kept oozing out of the hunter's mouth.

"Shut up," Sam's father told the man.

Sam's dad winced in pain as he tried to stand, but his twisted ankle wouldn't do him any favors.

Seeing the man this close, with no helmet, Will became acutely aware of what an awful thing he'd done. He'd forced this man and his wife to watch their son's beheading. *He must think I'm a monster.*

"I didn't kill your son," Will blurted out.

The hatred in the man's eyes frightened Will.

"I found him like that. I swear. I know I shouldn't have pretended he was alive. I know that was messed up. But I just had to get out. I'm—sorry. I so —"

"It was the hog," Sam's dad said.

"What?"

"You don't remember asking for a wild hog for a party?"

Of course Will did. He remembered the moment Gates had come up with the idea. He'd been so excited he'd thrown a champagne bottle against the wall in celebration.

"A kid that graduated yesterday . . . he told me he saw the hog attack Sam and rip his thr—" The man clamped his jaw shut, choking on emotion. He swallowed hard and continued. "I know it wasn't you, but I still don't like you or what you did. If you're going to stay on this farm, you're going to have to prove you're someone worth trusting."

Sam's dad stood with a pained grunt and limped off.

Will shouted after him, "I will."

"Hey," David said. "Breakfast."

Will opened his eyes and sat up on his cot. The smell of freshly tilled soil and manure, and trees and flowers, soothed the inside of his nostrils like the steam of a hot bath. The low whirr of summer crickets filled his ears. The day already felt warm, and sunlight had stretched its way to where he'd planted his toes in the grass below. He smiled and looked around. All the other cots under the tarp, in these emergency sleeping quarters, were empty.

"I guess I slept in."

"We start early around here," David said. "I just came from a security committee meeting about stepping up our security measures. Last night was a real wake-up call. Sam's dad already has plans for how to strengthen our whole operation."

He placed a wooden bowl in Will's lap and handed him his daily meds with water in a tin camping cup.

"Thanks," Will said. He swallowed his meds and set the cup aside.

"Normally I like to start the day with fresh scrambled eggs, but all the chickens are dead. We'll find new ones though. Just one more thing on the list."

"Morning, David," a woman said as she walked by with a pitchfork. Her hands were calloused and respectably filthy.

"Morning, Carol." When she was gone, David smiled at Will. "That's Bobby Corning's mom."

Will twisted his face. "For real? Does she know her son calls himself Jackal?"

David grinned. "She's the nicest lady. She makes those corn meal pancakes from scratch. Best thing you've ever had."

Will looked down at the bowl in his lap. Three little yellow pancakes sat snuggled up with each other, glistening with a thin caramel glaze of syrup. His stomach tugged at him. He dug into the pancakes with a fork and began shoveling. Creamy sweetness coated his tongue.

"Oh my God," Will said.

David arched his eyebrow. "Homemade butter."

"This is the best thing I've ever had in my entire life. Ever in my whole, entire life. How could someone make something as great as this and as awful as Bobby?"

David laughed. Will kept chomping through his breakfast. It was only as he reached the last few bites that he began to soak in what was happening beyond the shadow of the tent. Parents were working diligently everywhere he looked. There weren't many of them, maybe a couple more than he'd seen the night before, but it seemed like they'd already done the work of a hundred people. As Will's eyes traveled across the golden expanse of the farm, he could already see the evidence of the previous night's siege disappearing. Parts of the building had been damaged by grenade blasts. One of the massive steel plates that kept the school sealed up had been detached completely, but a group of fathers was already standing in front of it, trying to figure out how to reattach it. Plants had already been replanted where grenades had made craters. The small herd of cattle and goats, each in their own little pen, seemed content, leisurely chewing grass. The massive vegetable garden, where the parking lot had been torn up, looked unbothered.

"These people are machines," Will said, licking his fork. He put the bowl aside.

"They care," David said.

Will looked at his brother. He knew that serious face. It used to piss him off. He had always thought it was self-important and stupid, but that viewpoint seemed immature now. David was right. These parents wouldn't have been here, risking getting killed like they had last night, busting their asses like they were now, if they didn't care. He could see what he could never understand inside—they were regular people doing the best they possibly could under the shittiest circumstances. They'd occupied McKinley for half a year, but what they'd produced was impressive.

Near the parking lot garden, a team of moms was sorting through crates of fresh produce and cardboard boxes of supplies, making organized piles of cans in the grass. They distributed everything into battered plastic tubs that were on the crane pallet. They were prepping for a food drop. Two of the moms stepped away from their work to take a break. They shared a heartfelt hug.

"How often does this place get attacked?" Will said.

"That was the first time since I've been here. Pale Ridge hasn't seen too many homesteaders yet. From the wall, we've spotted the occasional RV or truck passing through town. Those guys last night are the first to stick around in a long time."

"Will there be more?"

"Maybe. People are moving back to Colorado since the military did their purge of infected. But the good news is we don't have to be here forever. We only have to last as long as the virus dies out inside McKinley, right? There's only so many people left inside."

Will nodded. He was only thinking of one. And if what David had told him was true, that Gates was dead, then he didn't have to worry about Lucy too badly. She had the Sluts.

"We just have to hold out until then," David said. "Thank God the parents planted as soon as they arrived. There's nothing more to be found from neighboring towns anymore. I know what you must think of Mr. Howard, but the guy had a plan for when the truck shipments got fewer and further between. We've got to be self-sufficient. Especially if we're going to have to be a fortress in the final days."

Will started to get sucked into a vortex of worry about how many other people like the grenade gang might eventually call Pale Ridge home again.

David put his hand on Will's shoulder. "Hey," he said. "We've been through a lot. We'll get through this too."

Will nodded. "Yeah, we will."

"We'll be watching cable on the couch before you know it."

Will laughed.

"You two!" Will and David looked over to see Sam's dad watching them. He leaned on a cane. David cringed and shot Will a worried look.

"Shit, here we go. Let me do the talking, okay? I'm in good with him," David said, then waved to Sam's dad.

"Will, I've got a special job for you. Think you can handle it?" Sam's dad said.

Will nodded and stood.

"Get your brother and follow me," Sam's dad said to Will.

David looked at Will, baffled. Will hadn't told him about

saving Sam's dad's life the night before, and clearly no one else had.

"'Get your brother'?" David muttered.

Will grinned. He couldn't help it. He loved when David was shocked. Will gave David a semi-gentle shove forward.

"You heard the guy. Get moving, slacker."

3

THREE CANDLES BY VIOLENT'S HEAD. THEY were the only light source in the small room. Lucy stood by the door. Violent hadn't noticed her yet. Asymmetrical swelling warped the shape of the Slut leader's head. Her breathing was shallow. They'd made her a bed on the floor out of all the gang's pillows, near an air vent in the wall so it would blow gently on her face. They'd thought maybe the filtered air would be better for her. Violent looked weak and vulnerable on the floor. Her health had been going downhill fast since the brawl with the Saints. The brawl that Lucy'd gotten them all into.

Her eyes bulged like two plums. Her head was wrapped in a white terry cloth towel, but red had soaked through. Her injuries were severe. Lucy knew Violent was human like the rest of them, but she carried herself with such an air of invincibility that Lucy had come to believe it was true. This seemed like a trick, a practical joke, that Violent was damaged and defeated. It didn't seem possible.

Her plum eyes opened and she looked at Lucy.

"You asked to see me?" Lucy said.

"C'mere."

Lucy approached with reluctance. She was frightened of what Violent would say. She'd never imagined this would happen. The other Sluts didn't want her talking to Violent. They were furious with her for getting their beloved leader so badly hurt in a brawl over a boy. Each girl had made sure to tell Lucy their version of the story—and list their personal injuries, all to get the point across about how badly she'd screwed up. After Lucy had escaped with Will, Gates and Violent had tangled and Violent had quickly lost the upper hand. Gates had slammed Violent's head into the floor over and over, and hadn't stopped until long after her eyes had rolled back in her head, and her arms had gone to rubber. The fact that Lucy had killed Gates was the only thing keeping the Sluts from ripping her apart. She was sure of it.

Lucy knelt by her leader's side. She took Violent's hand in hers. It was cold. She held it between her hands to warm it.

"I need to talk to you," Violent said. Her voice warbled. The authoritative bass she spoke with was gone, as was the forceful diction. Her voice had a childlike tremor to it.

"I'm here."

"I think this is it for me," Violent said.

"No, don't say that."

"I can feel it going away."

"You're imagining it. You're not going anywhere. I need you here." Lucy started crying. Saying the words out loud made her understand how much she depended on Violent, how much she drew strength from her. All the Sluts did. "The girls need you too."

Violent sighed, and Lucy could hear a gurgle in her windpipe.

"Doesn't change anything," she said.

"It's my fault," Lucy said.

"Lucy, shut up."

"Okay."

"I'm scared, Lucy. I'm really scared."

Lucy froze. This wasn't right. Violent didn't get scared. Sluts weren't supposed to.

"There's nothing to be scared of," Lucy said through a choked throat.

"I don't want this to be the end."

Lucy nodded. She didn't know what to say.

"I couldn't tell any of the others," Violent said. "They wouldn't understand. But you do."

But I don't, Lucy wanted to scream. *Please go back to being the old Violent.* She wanted her to sit up, shrug this off, and ask, "What's for dinner?"

"You've always reminded me of me," she said.

"How is that possible?" Lucy said.

"I used to be like you before all this. Soft. Sensitive. Worried about everything."

"I don't believe it."

"That's my secret. I still am that girl. I'm scared, Lucy. All the time."

"No, you're not. You're the most confident person I know."

Violent gripped her wrist. With a burst of strength, she yanked Lucy in close. Face-to-face. Sweat streaked Violent's pulsing temples. Her mouth couldn't decide on a position. Her pupils shivered.

"I'm too young to die," Violent said, on the edge of crying.

"Please don't say that."

"Help me, Lucy."

"I don't know what to do."

"What's going to happen to me?"

Violent moaned through a raspy throat. She held out her arms to Lucy. She wanted Lucy to hug her. Lucy hesitated from the shock, but as she went to hug her, Violent collapsed. She slumped facedown on the floor.

"I need help!" Lucy hollered.

The door whipped open and Sophia shot in. Sluts piled into the small room. They pulled Lucy away from Violent. Lips got ahold of Lucy and shoved her toward the door.

"Out," Lips said. She stared at Lucy with murder eyes.

Lucy ran out of the room, to the cafeteria dining hall. Black eyes, bloody lips, and scraped tits all around her. None of the girls was happy to see her. Lucy hung by herself in the corner.

It was only twenty minutes later that Sophia came shuffling into the dining hall. The bruising around Sophia's broken nose was purple and black, and her cheeks puffed out from the swelling, stretching her skin until it was shiny. Sophia blinked as she stared at Lucy, and when she spoke, her voice was cold as a gravestone.

"Her heart stopped beating," Sophia swallowed. "We couldn't get it back."

Everyone lost it, Lucy included. There was no Slut bravado, only grief. Girls started hugging, some dropped to the floor in agony. Lucy spotted Raunch and went in for a big hug. Raunch straight-armed her, palm to the chest. Raunch's tears soaked into the bandage for the severe gouge that now split her cheek. There was no love in her eyes. Lucy wandered to some of the other girls, but no one in the cafeteria would hug her. The picture was clear. Lucy didn't deserve a place in this mourning. She snuck off to the bathroom to cry alone.

"You sleep out here tonight," Lips said later, when it was time for bed.

The rest of the Sluts retired to the kitchen to sleep together, swaddled by the heat of the ovens. Lucy lay on a foldout table in the wide, empty room, where every creak of the table echoed, and she wished she had a blanket. The only thing that kept her company was her anguish over Violent, and one nagging question. If Violent's confidence had been fake all this time, if she was just as vulnerable and scared as the rest of them, what hope did Lucy have?

The thought kept her up for hours.

In the morning, Lucy made sure to get up before anyone else, stow her table away, and do some general chores before the rest of the girls woke up. She knew she had a lot to make up for.

When the Sluts filtered out of the kitchen to start their day, they ignored her and the work she had done. Things puttered to life as if she weren't there. Pots and pans clanged as Samantha prepared breakfast. Girls stowed their mattress men away, then trudged to the bathroom to take sink and bucket showers. Their faces were grim, but they went about their chores with a sense of purpose, like they'd been given a pep talk in the kitchen before they'd emerged. Raunch swept the cardboard wrestling mat where self-defense training would be commencing shortly, and paused to clean her prescription basketball goggles with her shirt. Lucy wondered if she should go over to help. She was afraid to talk to Raunch, to any of them.

Lips emerged from the kitchen with a full trash bag in her hand. Her other arm was in a sling made out of a pair of jeans. She looked at Lucy, and the look wasn't hate-filled like

Lucy expected. Lips's poor excuse for a mouth, that crack in her face, wasn't frowning as usual, or pinched up in disgust either. It was a flat line. She walked up to Lucy and held out the heavy trash bag.

"Take this out," Lips said.

Lucy could suddenly breathe again. This was a good sign. She'd do their chores for weeks, if that's what it took.

"Thanks," Lucy said.

"Just do it, fuckhead. No talking."

Same old Lips. *Best not to push it,* Lucy figured. She took the heavy black bag, opened the cafeteria door, and carried the trash out to the pile in the hallway outside. As soon as she swung the bag into the pile, she felt a wave of loneliness rush through her, and she started to cry. About Violent, about Will graduating early, about no one wanting to hug her, and all her friends shunning her, and a tiny bit because crying felt good.

She had to stop. She knew that when she opened the door to the cafeteria and walked back in, she had to show them that she was a Slut, and unafraid. Those girls still lived by Violent's persona, whether it had been real or not. She'd never tell any of them what Violent shared with her last night. Violent wouldn't want that. Lucy wiped her slick cheeks.

"Pull it together, what the fuck," she said.

She let her breathing slow down. She turned to face the cafeteria doors and assumed as confident a posture as she could manage. She grabbed the door handle.

It was locked.

She pulled again. It wouldn't budge.

"Hey," Lucy said loudly.

She knocked. Silence.

Lucy paced. "Very funny," she hollered.

She was greeted again with a longer silence. She knocked harder. Again, there was no response.

Something caught Lucy's eye in the trash pile.

The cardboard sheath she'd made for David's machete, the one she'd had with her when she'd joined the Sluts, poked out of the trash bag that she had just thrown into the pile. Lucy rushed to the bag and pulled out the sheath. The words *THE LONERS* were still written across it in silver thumbtacks, just like she had made it. She recognized something else in the garbage bag, her old, dirty gray sneakers. Lucy pushed them aside and began rifling through the bag.

It was full of everything she owned.

4

HILARY WAS FILTHY. SHE DIDN'T KNOW HOW long she'd been down in the basement, knee-high in the school's trash. Everything seemed like a blur since Lucy had flushed her tooth down the toilet. Maybe she shouldn't have dragged this Freak girl down to the basement and yanked out her tooth. Maybe she had gotten a little carried away. Just thinking about Lucy now had her grinding her jaw. She had to calm down.

She paced amid the garbage. Something jabbed through the sole of her flats and poked her heel. She jumped and lifted her foot. A giant piece of glass had sliced through and ruined her shoe.

"Shit!" she said.

Why was this happening to her? She couldn't go back to the gym with ruined shoes, a filthy dress, and stinking like a gutter person. She'd already lost people's respect when Terry had taken away her privileges, like her private bedroom and her solo swim. The Pretty Ones would laugh at her. And once they started laughing at her instead of fearing her, she would never get them back under her thumb.

Hilary honestly couldn't figure out how she'd gotten into this situation.

"I mean, is it me?" she said. "Did I do this?"

Hilary turned and looked down at the Freak girl on her back, still strapped to the tipped chair. She was passed out. Her gag was stained brown with old blood. The new, raw gap between her teeth made her look thirty. The bags under her eyes weren't helping either. But just because she was ugly, didn't mean she had no brain. Hilary squatted down over her, lifted her head up, and untied her gag. The girl's eyes fluttered awake. When she saw Hilary over her, she flinched.

"Do you think it's my fault that I'm down here?" Hilary said. "Because it feels like I've hit bottom."

Hilary waited for the girl to answer, as patiently as she could, because the little gnat was really taking her fucking time.

"Just tell me," Hilary said. "I can take it."

"P-please let me go."

"Oh for fuck's sake," Hilary said, and threw up her arms. She walked away from the girl.

"Please! I'll do anything you want," the Freak said.

The girl kept pleading, but Hilary tuned her out. She was good at that.

Hilary's mood brightened when she saw a pair of calfskin boots sticking out of the side of a hill of trash. They were six sizes too big, but they were relatively clean, and she could use them. Her shoes were garbage now. She grabbed the boots and pulled. This triggered a mini-avalanche of trash. Along with the cascading refuse came a flood of cockroaches, and a human body. Hilary yelped and jumped back. The body of a boy slid out of the hill of filth and rolled to her feet. The boots had an owner.

She covered her mouth in shock, and danced away from the hissing scramble of roaches.

The dead boy had white hair and a white beard. She'd seen him before. On the quad a few times. Next to Gates. He was a Saint. And someone had cut his scalp off. She could see the cool quartz of his bare skull. His skin was yellowing, and there was a maggot wiggling along the lower eyelid of his left eye. Hilary turned away and closed her eyes.

She couldn't get sick on her dress. That would only make everything worse. Hilary turned away. She didn't look at the boy's face again. She focused on his boots. She grabbed one with both hands. With a little back-and-forth, she worked the boot off. Something slid out of it and landed neatly on the floor.

She shook her head. What she was seeing was impossible.

She picked the impossible thing up. It was ice-cold in her hands. She clicked it open.

She laughed.

It wasn't impossible. It was exactly right. Now everything made sense. This was why she'd been brought so low, down into the filth. To find this. Her destiny.

The cutest little revolver she'd ever seen. Fully loaded.

Hilary clomped into the gym in her oversized boots. Her legs must have looked like saplings in full-size planters. Her white dress had gone brown from sweat and muck. She stank so bad she could smell herself, but Hilary didn't care about any of it. Let the Pretty Ones look. Let Varsity. She had the world in her handbag.

Her dad had shown her a gun like this before. He used to show her lots of guns. It was called a Saturday night special. He'd referred to it as a lady gun, and he'd been pissed that he'd bought it for her mom and she'd never seemed to care. He'd said that when Hilary was old enough, he'd give the damn thing to her. But that never happened. He'd walked out on Hilary and her mother, and had taken the gun with him. One more promise the guy hadn't kept. But she had her own gun now, and it was going to change everything.

Loud chatter echoed across the basketball court, bouncing off the walls and the high, bannered ceilings. The gym was full of kids from every gang. She wanted to puke. Terry had been kicking around the idea of opening up the pool to the rest of the school and charging people to swim. It looked like he had finally done it. They were lined up all across the gym floor, towels in hand, waiting for their chance to use the pool. Blue hair peppered the line, and black and red and rainbow. Not since the raid on Sam's food pile had there been this many other gangs in the gym. Their filthy hands touching the walls, filthier feet streaking her floor. It wasn't right.

"Oh my God."

A group of Pretty Ones was staring at Hilary. Every single jaw was hanging open, except Linda's. Tall Linda with the thick hair. She was grinning like someone had just handed her a bag of diamonds.

"You look like shit," she said, then giggled. The other girls dared to laugh with her.

No one would have dared to talk to her like that when Sam had been alive. Linda had been getting out of hand again.

"Nice boots," Linda said. "What did you trade for them, your self-respect?"

The girls laughed louder now. Hilary smiled at Linda. She could tell it made Linda nervous.

"You think you're such a rebel, don't you, Linda?"

Linda rolled her eyes for the other girls' sake.

"I'm so disappointed in all of you," Hilary said. "I guess I'll have to teach you a lesson."

The girls stopped laughing and looked to one another. They'd be so easy to herd again. She walked away, left them hanging. It was just what she wanted, their eyes on her when she talked to Terry.

She found the Varsity leader sitting at the top of the bleachers on a portion he'd carpeted in mocha-colored, faux alpaca fur that he'd ordered through Gates. Terry gave a wave to a Geek boy with a pair of green pigtails, who was next in line for the pool. Two Varsity guards were manning the pool entrance. When one wet kid would leave, they'd wave a new kid forward from the line. That kid would pass off a food item to the guards and then head down to the pool.

"Hilary!" Terry said with a smile when he saw her.

"Some business you've got going here."

"Genius, isn't it? All this time we've been sitting on a gold mine."

"It used to be that Varsity took whatever food they wanted. They didn't pimp themselves out."

Terry frowned. "You look like you need a shower, sweetie."

"Funny, I used to have one all to myself, but someone took it away from me."

Terry shook his head like the condescending dick that he was, and said, "You've got to get into the spirit of things around here, Hil. You're in real danger of becoming obsolete. If you're not careful, people might decide they don't need you around."

"Is that a threat?" Hilary said, loud enough for everyone to hear. Heads turned.

"You could take it that way, sure," Terry said. He looked to the Varsity guys sitting up and down the bleachers, legs spread and kicked out. They grinned back at him.

"Bad idea," Hilary said and pulled the pistol from her handbag. She held it up for everyone to see.

For a moment, everyone went quiet. She had the attention of the whole room. Then, the gym erupted. And not with screams. Laughter socked her in the ears. Kids in line started to shout at her and call her nasty things. They stuck their hands down their pants. They were vile. All of them. There wasn't enough chlorine in the world to cleanse the pool of the dirt in the creases of their necks, behind their ears, in their stewing rear ends. It was all in her water. She'd be marinating in them.

How dare they laugh.

But they'd seen Saints with guns before. Guns with no bullets.

"You're banned," Terry said, and got up. He started a slow walk down the bleachers as if this little game had gotten out of hand, and it was finally time for him to put a stop to it. "If you ever set foot in my gym again—"

Hilary shot Terry. The gun bucked in her hand. It sounded like a car fell from the ceiling and hit the floor. Hilary's whole arm vibrated. Everybody hit the deck.

The line to the pool tried to scatter and escape the gym. She leveled the gun at the crowd and they all froze. Some dropped to the ground with their hands splayed, pleading. Hilary's insides tingled. The gun led her and she listened.

The gym rippled with screams, but when they died down, only one stayed at full blast. Terry was floundering on the bleachers, clutching his foot, trying to stop the blood that was pouring over his hand and onto his alpaca rug. Varsity guys ran to him, and Hilary let them.

She had five bullets left.

"I got a whole locker full of ammo," she shouted. "And I *want* to use it."

Nobody moved. She looked around the gym. No one dared to make eye contact with her. Behind her, she could hear Terry crying. She felt wild and powerful. She flashed her fury at Linda and the rest of the girls, who were staring and holding each other. They'd forgotten what it meant to fear her, but they'd remembered with the flick of a trigger.

"Shut the pool door. Now."

Linda and another Pretty One, Britt, ran to the door. The Varsity guards stepped out of their way. They swung the door shut. Hilary would deal with the swimmers below later. She liked seeing Linda tremble and look to the Varsity boys for help. They wanted to leap behind their boys. They craved protection. Hilary laughed to herself. She realized her days of manipulating a boy to get what she wanted were over. She didn't need anyone anymore, she had the gun. People would have to try their best to seduce her, not the other way around.

"It looks like we've suffered a terrible injury here in Varsity," Hilary said. "So, I'm going to have to pick up the slack. I'm in charge now."

She twirled her hair with the barrel of the gun.

"And while we're at it, let's just put me in charge of everybody. That's for the best. You can still have your gangs. I don't want to mess with a good thing, but think of them like states. And I'm president. Except for, I guess there was no election, so . . . Let's just say I'm Queen. Call me that. I like that."

"She shot me . . . ," Terry muttered. "You shot me . . ."

"You shot me, *Queen*," Hilary said, correcting him. "Now, like I was saying, pool time is over. Everybody, get the hell out and spread the word—if I want something done, you better do it, or I'll put a bullet in your head."

People started to stand, cautiously. With a swing of the gun, Hilary motioned them toward the exit.

"You can leave now."

They ran.

When a Geek girl hurried past, Hilary's eyes were drawn to her homemade, silver-sequin high heels.

"STOP," Hilary yelled. She pointed the gun at the girl, and the girl froze.

"No . . . ," the girl pleaded. "Not me."

"Leave your shoes. And get the hell out of my face."

The girl nodded frantically as she yanked off her shoes. She dropped them at Hilary's feet and scurried out barefoot. Hilary kicked off her too-big boots and slipped into the high heels. They were so snug and they looked to die for with the matching silver snub-nose in her hand.

Hilary sighed. Things were looking up.

5

LUCY DIDN'T DARE STEP FOOT ONTO THE
quad. It was no place to go alone. And more than that, she'd
killed somebody there. The mud was dry from the cooking
sun but still torn up by the Harley's fat tire tracks. The earth
had been thrashed into long six-inch-high ridges and valleys.
She could still make out the shape of her own body where
she'd lain down in the quad, after Gates had died, and stared
into the rain.

Lucy stood in the shadow of the south entrance, just inside
the hall. A gust of wind blew in and flapped the towel she wore
over her head like a sheikh. It was tied off with a headband to
cover her red hair. The lockout from the cafeteria that morning had been permanent, and she was lucky the girls hadn't
shaved her head. She wasn't a Slut anymore. She wasn't anything. Just a Scrap wearing a black trash bag as a dress.

She stared up at the roofline, and waited for Will to appear.

It had been hours and he hadn't come yet. But he could come. It was possible.

Another gust of wind flattened Lucy's trash bag to her front. Leaves blew into the hall from the quad. She could hear their dry scratch across the linoleum floor behind her. A woman patrolled the roof's perimeter in workout clothes. She wore a scuba mask and a petite tank. A rifle was slung over her shoulder. The parents were using rubber bullets now. They weren't going to tolerate another hostage situation. They seemed to want to make it abundantly clear that they were in charge. Lucy hadn't been shot with one yet, but she'd seen a Skater get hit. The boy had lain in the dirt, squirming and crying like a baby for twenty minutes.

Lucy heard noise behind her. People approaching. She ducked around the corner and into the quad. She stood with her back to the wall, facing the quad, just feet from the hallway's opening.

Saints poured out from the hallway. Lucy felt her grip on the gathered plastic of her trash bag grow slippery with sweat. Ten, twenty, thirty morose Saints came trudging out, looking like they'd slept in their clothes. A hungover preppy parade. The Saints barely lifted their feet as they shuffled toward the center of the quad. Lucy stayed ready to run if any of them glanced her way. None of them did. Their heads were all bowed low, except four guys who shared the burden of carrying a long, taped-up box.

A cardboard coffin.

Time slowed as Lucy saw into the coffin. The inside was filled with crumpled-up pieces of white printer paper. They reminded her of carnations. Gates's dead face rose out of the sea of white paper like a lone, rosy-cheeked island. Some Saint girl had blown out her makeup kit, covering his bluish-gray dead skin with a sun-kissed flesh tone. Despite the approximation of healthy skin, Gates's face had lost whatever fullness life gave it, and it was as if the flesh of his face was melting off the bone.

The memory of him the other night, on top of her in the rain, with his pants off, trying to strangle her, would never leave her mind. She wasn't sorry to see him dead, but the Saints were.

They walked like they were wading through honey. Their heads seemed too heavy for their tired necks to support. They carried Gates to the center of the quad and set him down. When the last of the Saints exited the hallway, Lucy ducked back into the hall and watched from the shadows. As the procession passed she kept her head turtled inside the towel. If anyone had seen her, they hadn't seen her face.

A Saint girl with short wispy white hair stood by Gates's coffin, her puffed eyes dripping tears down onto the crumpled white paper. Lucy had seen her before. Her name was Lark. She had always been hanging around Gates, or off Will. She looked like she'd been crying for hours.

"Did you love him?" Lark said, in a voice squeezed tight with emotion.

The Saints answered back with a resounding, "Yes."

"So did I," Lark said.

Her face was clenched like she was being electrocuted. Lucy remembered seeing Lark with a dislocated jaw at the Saint–Slut battle. It looked like it pained her to talk.

Lark pulled out a black-and-white composition notebook she'd been holding under her arm. She opened it to a book-marked page.

"Gates had a statement prepared in case of his death," Lark said.

The Saints gasped like she'd said she'd brought stone tablets down from the mountaintop.

Lark cleared her throat.

"'S up, fags."

The Saints laughed.

"I guess I'm dead," she continued, "which is hard for me to imagine. Whatever took me out would have to be something pretty major. I hope I went down fighting two bears. Or in a bazooka fight. Was I at least on fire?"

More laughs from the Saints. The smiles their fallen leader's words created were quick to fade. Their grief was too profound to be reversed with a few jokes from beyond the grave.

"I don't know when you'll be reading this, hopefully never. I'm writing this in the sewer underneath city hall. In

Broomfield. In case we end up hiding out in any other sewers under any other city halls."

The Saints nodded and smiled.

"The rest of you are eating dinner now. I'm watching you laugh. Telling stories about the summer before all this shit happened. I feel so grateful to have all of you, and to have had the opportunity to lead this group for a long time. I've done my best to keep us all alive. I'm going to keep going as long as I can, and try to make it fun as shit along the way. But let's be real, my number could come up tomorrow. So I figured I had to write this letter to all of you. The group has to stay together. We are a family. Celebrate being alive together. Throw the biggest going-away party Colorado has ever seen for me, and tell stories about me till the sun rises. Please don't forget me. I'll never forget any of you. Peace, fuck, barf, love. Your pal, Gates."

In one motion, Lark ripped the page out of the notebook. She fished a lighter out of the waist of her tights, and set the page on fire.

"Good-bye, baby," Lark said, and dropped the flaming page into the coffin. The flames quickly ate their way across the crumpled paper until the entire coffin was ablaze. The tall fire churned out clouds of black smoke that snaked up into the sky, before getting swirled and spread thin by the gusting winds.

Lucy retreated from the quad as fast as she could. *You*

aren't supposed to go to the funeral of someone you killed. She felt nauseous. She'd ended someone's life, and she'd really believed she should feel different, changed somehow, but she felt eerily the same. She saw their anguish, and she felt awful to be the cause of it, but if she was in the same situation again, she wouldn't do any different. She didn't know what kind of person that made her. Bad, she guessed.

At the top of a flight of stairs, she climbed up onto the handrail and removed the air vent cover grille above. A string was discreetly tied around one of the grille's louvered slats, preventing it from falling to the floor. Lucy lifted herself up into the darkness of the metal air duct, and crawled through the square tunnel. She reached the grille that she was looking for and pushed till it popped out.

She'd made it. Maxine's secret greenhouse. This would be her new home. The room that no one who was left in McKinley knew about. The room where she'd lost her virginity to Will. It was dark, but by the light that streamed in through the window, she could see that the white flower on the windowsill was still alive, its petals open, white, and fresh.

Lucy needed water. She'd finished the water from the spray bottle meant for Maxine's flower the night before. And that was the last of it. She needed food too. The waves of hunger would take hold of her belly, but if she rode them out, they'd fade for another hour or two. Until they'd come back worse.

Still, that was better than venturing out of her hidden room. At least in here, she was safe.

She stared at a piece of paper in her hand. It was a Xerox of Lucy's and Will's faces, nose to nose, their cheeks smushed into the copier glass. The image was overexposed and grainy, but they were both grinning like fools. They'd stuck their heads on the machine and made it on the one night they'd stayed in this room together. The last night he'd been here.

It was as if that night had never happened. Will was gone, people were dead, and all she had left of it was a piece of paper. She missed him like crazy. She wished he had never graduated, and it was just the two of them living in this room together. Then she wouldn't be so afraid. Lucy touched his face on the Xerox.

She tucked the image in her pocket and climbed on top of the table. She pulled herself into the metal air duct. She brought the empty spray bottle with her. If she didn't find food and water soon, she'd end up being too weak to do anything, and she'd die for sure. The duct was cold and dark. The metal popped and burped as she moved her weight across it. She came to the vent cover that opened to the stairwell, and pressed her face to the vent.

Four Skater boys were heading down the stairs. When they reached the landing below and turned the corner to go down the next flight, Lucy began to unfasten the vent cover. She heard a rumble up the stairwell. The Skaters turned on their heels and hightailed it back up the stairs and down the hall. A moment later, Lucy saw what they were running from.

Varsity flooded the landing. They poured out from around the corner and ascended the stairs, right under her nose. They kept coming, a river of yellow hair, fifty at least. It had to be half their gang, all walking together. Freshly dyed and in uniform.

The sight of a gang that size made her acutely aware that she was alone. She couldn't believe she was a Scrap again. Her first time as a Scrap, after the Pretty Ones had kicked her out, had been horrible, but it had only lasted a few hours before David had entered her life as her protector. The other girls in the Loners had told her stories of what it was like for girl Scraps, and they'd painted a frightening picture. Boys offering protection in return for sex. Offering food for sex. Boys finding any leverage possible to get you to spread your legs. And if you made the mistake of actually doing it? They'd all know. They'd tell each other, and after that, they'd never stop hounding you, and they'd offer less and less in return each time.

That wasn't going to be her.

She'd steal. She'd fight in the food drops by herself. She'd do what she had to do. The Sluts had taught her to be tough, to not take any shit She'd changed while she was with them. She knew she had. She was still the tougher, braver version of herself. She just had to keep repeating that in her head.

6

"GET HIM!" DAVID SHOUTED.

He'd just made a dive to grab a gopher, but all he had to show for it was a fist full of kale. He'd worked hard to make sure having one eye wasn't a handicap, but there were times when he couldn't count on his depth perception, and this was one of them. The little brown bastard was bounding through the crop and if he made it to the football field of wheat, they'd lose him for another day or two. Which meant more plants ruined by his little, gnawing rodent teeth.

Thankfully, Will was on the job. Where David had fallen, Will had closed in. He was moving at a good clip, only a foot behind the animal.

In the past month, Will had gotten great at catching gophers, among other things. The truth was that David was in awe of his little brother. He'd manage to charm most of the parents, Sam's dad included, with his scrappiness and his humor. He'd been afraid they'd have a rocky relationship like they'd had in McKinley, but it wasn't the case. They were getting along and Will was coming into his own right in front of David's eyes.

The parents had enforced a regimented food drop, where every gang received their food separately, and no fighting was allowed. It had been rough getting it going, but now the food drops were violence-free, and going off without a hitch. He could barely believe it, peaceful food drops. David let out a contented sigh. This was as good as life had been for a long time.

Will made his lunge, but the gopher made a snap turn and dove into a freshly dug hole. Dry dust engulfed Will as he rolled onto his back and shouted in frustration.

"I had him!" he said.

A throaty cackle came from the wall.

"Screw you, Bertie," Will said and threw up a middle finger at the man doing the laughing.

Bertie was the farm's only prisoner, the hunter Will had taken down with the pickax, which had become everyone's favorite story to tell about the night of the siege. Especially since Bertie had proved himself to be such a miserable excuse for human life. He lived in a custom cell in one of the tractor trailers that made up the outer farm wall. The parents had done him a favor by giving him a big, steel mesh window, so he wasn't in the dark all day, but Bertie didn't give a damn about the view. All he used it for was heckling.

"I been watching you two dumbasses for weeks, chasing gophers, setting pillowy, lil' pussy traps. All you're doing is wasting time while your food dies. And then you die. Why're you killing yourself when there's an easy answer right in front'a ya?" he said. His voice was a nasally assault, with the timbre of a chain saw.

"We're not shooting them," Will said as he dusted himself off.

Bertie cackled again. "That's the rat in you talking, kid. One disease carrier sympathizing with another. Hey, one-eye, you sure little brother here is not still infected? 'Cause it sounds like his brain still is."

Will started walking toward Bertie's cell. David moved to stop him.

"Let it go," David told his brother.

"You want me to come in there with a pickax again, old man?" Will said. "Maybe I should just finish the job."

"You don't got it in you, kid. None of you bleeding hearts do. That's why you're up on this hill, all scared and waiting. You know what's gotta happen."

"Oh, yeah, asshole? What's that?"

"You're sitting on a balloon full of poison! How long till it pops? You gotta burn 'em. Roast 'em. Put a bullet through every one of their heads, you pussies. You know that's the only way. You're just too blind to see it."

David patted Will on the back.

"Let's go," he said. It took a little tug, but he got Will to walk away from the wall.

"You're gonna kill us all," Bertie said to their backs.

David could feel the tension in Will's back, the urge to turn, but he kept walking.

"Ya hear me?" Bertie shouted.

"We did a heck of a job on that fence," David said to drown Bertie out.

Will looked up at the farm wall and the razor-wire-lined chain-link fence that gleamed atop it. Three crows sat along the fence not far from the front gate. The gate doors, which were welded patchworks of rusted sheet metal, wavy aluminum siding, and a few road signs, looked more like folk art, but they were as high as a castle gate.

"You mean *I* did a heck of a job," Will said. "All you did was 'supervise.'"

"Somebody's gotta be the brains in this family," David said. He laughed and tapped his eye patch. "Besides, I'm handicapped."

"Yeah, when it's handy."

David laughed again. The three crows flew from their perch, making the razor wire tremble at their takeoff. The guard on the wall, Mr. Miller, a bald man in green sweatpants, who had been David's music teacher in elementary school, turned to face the farm. He mumbled in a panic, then called out to the others, "Uh, someone's coming!"

Bertie didn't miss a beat from his cage. "They're coming for me! I told ya, didn't I? Ya bastards. Didn't I say? They're coming for me!"

Will shared a nervous look with David.

There was a rush to the wall from all over the farm. Parents wove through the labyrinth of single-lane paths that cut around the crops and gardens. Those closest to the wall were quick to get up it, with weapons ready. Jason Howard was already at Mr. Miller's side. He climbed to the metal bridge that passed over the gate and was also a checkpoint for interaction with anyone outside. Sam's dad began to talk to someone unseen below, on the other side of the wall.

David and Will passed the hog pen, and David snatched up a shovel that was leaning against the fence. He choked up tight on the tool, not quite sure what he was ready for, but ready nonetheless. Sam's dad turned back to face the farm.

"Open the gate."

David loosened up on the shovel. The parents nearest the gate unfastened the chain that was looped through its giant iron handles. They pulled the doors open. A black minivan idled in the drive. Its paint was flecked with white dings, and an ugly smash had pushed the custom grille guard up on one side, giving it a crooked smile. Five wide metal slats ran across the windshield and side windows like protective venetian blinds.

With a rev, the van cruised in. The parents shut the door

behind it. The van stopped, the driver-side door swung open, and a giant figure stepped out. The van seemed to sigh at the relief of no longer carrying its tremendous driver. The guy lifted a thick hand and gave David and Will a wave.

"Is that . . . ?" Will said.

Gonzalo. The ax-wielding Loner who could scare a Varsity with a sneer. He was even bigger than he used to be. He towered over the van, his shoulders level with its roof. David hadn't seen him in months. His hair was still a frizzy mop that hid his face, but it was shorter. He'd cut off the white.

David stabbed the shovel into the ground, and the brothers hurried to their old friend.

"Big man! Where you been?" David said.

"Up north," Gonzalo said.

"Did you find her?" David said.

Gonzalo shook his head, jutting his jaw in disappointment.

"Find who?" Will said. "Hold on, you two have seen each other since McKinley?"

It was a long story, and from a period that David had been avoiding telling Will about. A memory he wanted to forget. After he'd broken out of McKinley and escaped the hunters, he'd decided to head east, away from the Rockies, hoping that if he crossed the state line, he might be back in civilization again, and maybe there he could find someone sane who could help him help McKinley. Instead, what he found was more danger and more starvation.

After three weeks, he was living under a railroad bridge with a broken ankle, surviving on fish from a polluted stream and hiding out from a group of infected whom he'd watched torture and kill a hunter. He'd thought of Lucy nearly constantly and wished she were there to nurture and encourage him. He'd been so sure he'd die out there but Gonzalo had found him and taken him away. Gonzalo had been spending his time scouring the infected zone by himself, searching for his girlfriend, Sasha. He told David about what the parents were doing, and helped him get back to the school so he could join the effort.

That was the last time he'd talked to Gonzalo. Seeing him again, now, with Will, was a surprise treat, especially on a campus populated by fiftysomethings.

The three of them sat at a circular beige table under the blue dining tent. Sam's dad had just left them after inquiring about what Gonzalo had seen outside. He'd told Sam's dad "nothing much" but that wasn't what he was telling them now.

"There's a cure," Gonzalo said. He was chewing on a piece of venison jerky from the farm stock.

"What?" Will said. He gaped at Gonzalo. "Why didn't you say so?"

Gonzalo shrugged. "Figured you'd want to know first. You can tell who needs to know."

"So . . . ," David said. "They're handing this cure out or what?"

"I don't know the details, man. All I know is that people are saying that there is one. I was up in Nebraska. Tracked Sasha there, only it wasn't her. Dead ringer, though."

The corners of Gonzalo's mouth dipped. It was the only hint of disappointment he let on.

"This girl and the crew she was with were headed to Minnesota. Some famous research place there. A hospital or something in Rochester. They heard they had a cure for the virus—"

"They heard," David clarified.

Gonzalo finished his jerky and wiped his massive hands. "Yeah, heard. But it sounds pretty legit to me."

"You didn't go see for yourself?" Will said.

Gonzalo shook his head. "My girl's still out there, Willie. I gotta backtrack my trail until I catch her scent again. When I find her, then we'll go for the cure."

The big guy cleared his throat. David could have sworn he heard his voice crack with emotion.

"But nothing's distracting me till she's with me again. That's all I care about. David knows what I'm talking about."

Will gave David a piercing look. His face was tensed by a hint of that old jealousy David remembered from when Lucy had been in their everyday life. It had nearly torn them apart back in McKinley. And David wasn't about to let that happen again. Since Will had gotten out, things between David and his brother had been better than they'd ever been. The last thing he wanted was for some drivel he'd said about Lucy after his breakdown in the infected zone to ruin things. He didn't even know if he still felt that way about Lucy anymore, anyway.

"You'll find her. I know it," David said.

"Yeah, and when you do, we'll have the cure here, waiting for her," Will said.

David nodded along for Gonzalo's benefit, but Will seemed to sense that David was just humoring them.

"I'm serious," Will said to David. "We should go to Minnesota."

David glanced over at his brother.

"Uh, I don't know. That's pretty far to go on just a rumor. Half the trip, maybe more, is through the infected zone."

"So?"

"Well, it's dangerous," David said.

"It's dangerous here. It's dangerous everywhere. My first hour on the farm nearly got me blown up."

"Yeah, but . . . you haven't been out there," David said, looking to Gonzalo for support. He was a stone wall. Outside was Gonzalo's life. David didn't want to go back out there. He was scared, but he didn't want to tell them that.

"David, you're the one that said it's only a matter of time until we're outnumbered by people moving back to Pale Ridge. What if everyone inside hasn't graduated by then? A cure is a chance to better the odds, man. If everybody gets virus-free, then we've got no problems anymore. And how far is Minnesota anyway?"

"Twelve, fifteen-hour drive, something like that," Gonzalo said.

Will pointed at Gonzalo with a wild grin.

"Let's do it," he said. "We'd be heroes."

It was what David admired most about his brother. He had no fear of the unknown. Then again, too many times David had seen the brashness that came with it be Will's undoing. That was exactly what had tangled him up with Gates when David had been powerless to help. Watching that train wreck from above and then going on the missions to fulfill Gates's demands had been agonizing. But that was over now. They'd survived. And just as often David had seen Will's brashness morph into bravery, like when he had taken down Varsity single-handedly. Everything Will was saying now was right. If they retrieved a cure, all of this just might end happily.

"A fifteen-hour drive is nothing to scoff at," David said. "We'll need supplies we can't spare. Fuel we don't have. And we'll have to get more gas mask filters somewhere on the way. There's still infected out there. It's still a war zone."

"So, what are you saying?" Will said.

"If we could get all that," David said, "then . . . it's worth a shot."

Will clapped his hands with a big smile.

"Road trip!"

7

LUCY COULD HANDLE THE REST. SHE COULD
stomach the loneliness of her new life in her plant room. She could withstand the waves of sadness that washed over her without warning. She could deal with the fact that none of the gangs would let her join. And with the reality that she'd traded away everything she'd owned in the last few weeks. She'd made peace with becoming a thief, a beggar in disguise. The hunger dictated her morality, it negated her pride. She could handle all that. What she couldn't handle was what she held in her hand.

A positive pregnancy test.

She'd traded nearly everything she had left for it. Lucy squinted at the pink plus sign like it might be a mirage. The result seemed impossible, even though she knew it was the opposite. It was extremely possible. It was what happened when people had sex. They hadn't used any protection that night. This was happening because of what she'd done. She'd brought it on herself. Just like Violent's death, or getting kicked out of the Sluts.

Sometime in the future, somewhere other than here, maybe this news would have warmed her heart that there was a tiny person growing within her, but not here in McKinley, and not now, when she had no one. The responsibility felt like a tree trunk strapped to her shoulders. She was too young for this, too ill-equipped. Before the quarantine, she'd never even babysat.

Her heart started to thump, a film of sweat covered her body. She had to do something. She'd go crazy sitting and thinking about it in her plant room. She had to find food. Now more than ever. She had to start building up a supply for when she got too big to go back and forth through the vent.

Her hands trembled as she took her nose plugs off the windowsill. They were short sections of a thick plastic straw from a sports water bottle. Each was only a centimeter long, and she'd lined the outside in layers of masking tape to make them thicker. When she shoved them up into her nostrils, it changed the shape of her nose. It was wider, with chunkier nostrils, but she could still breathe. Next, she took two jelly bra inserts and stuck them in her cheeks. She'd found them in a backpack she'd stolen from a bathroom while the owner was in one of the stalls. She had cut the inserts down to fit right, but they successfully puffed out her cheeks and made her face seem rounder. She grabbed handfuls of moist soil from the jars by the wall, and smeared the dirt all over her face, her hands, and any exposed skin.

There was a handful of kids in school with real mental conditions, who wandered around in filthy clothes, looking confused, begging for food, and yelling at people who weren't there. Dickie Bellman would have been one of them, if he hadn't been shot down at Gonzalo's graduation. There was Mime Jerry, who stood by the same water fountain near the stairs to the basement, and he never stopped miming. Twenty-four/seven, you could always count on him being there, fighting to get out of a box, desperately, silently begging you to let him out. There was a cross-eyed boy who never stopped running through the halls of the school. There was another boy on the second floor by the auditorium who just sat in an open locker, smiling all day and staring into the distance. There was a girl who never wore pants, or underwear. She was always angry, and never seemed to understand anything you said to her. Once she'd broken a Skater girl's fingers who'd tried to help her out by brushing her hair. No one touched the girl after that. That was the sort of reputation Lucy was looking for now.

She crawled through the air duct to the hall. The middle of the day was the worst time to travel through the halls of McKinley, but Lucy needed to talk to a friend. She made her way to the library. Passersby avoided her like the plague, but she much preferred that to her actual reputation of the girl who got her gang leader killed. When she neared the library, she discovered Belinda cleaning out her locker in the hallway.

Seeing Belinda now, after weeks of loneliness and rejection, had a crippling effect on Lucy. She watched in awe as her old friend rifled through her locker, either chucking things onto the floor or into the small purple backpack she had with her. Her clothes were clean and unwrinkled. Belinda's face bloomed with happiness. There was something vivacious to the way she was sorting her locker. She was bubbling over with energy, and love, and hope—all feelings that Lucy couldn't seem to summon anymore.

"Belinda . . . ," Lucy dared to say, her syllables distorted by her overstuffed cheeks.

Belinda jerked with shock, and backed away at the sight of Lucy coming toward her. Lucy realized she had forgotten her disguise for a moment.

"Wait," she said. She pulled the spacers out of her nose, and the jelly cutlets out of her mouth. "It's me, Lucy."

She saw the truth click into place on Belinda's face.

"Oh my God, Lucy. Oh, baby. Oh no. What happened to you?" Belinda said.

Lucy wanted to tell her no, this was only a disguise, that she wasn't this low, this dirty, this driven to the edge, but as soon as she thought it she started to cry. She was all those things, only in a disguise. She told Belinda everything. She told her about the baby, about starving, about living in hiding, about the feeling that the world was collapsing in all around her.

Belinda rubbed her back as Lucy spilled her feelings. Belinda bit her lip. She told her all the nice girlfriend things that she was supposed to say: that this would be okay, that this was probably meant to be, that she'd only grow stronger from it, and that Lucy was too nice a person for this to be the end of her story. All that stuff.

"I feel so much better just knowing I have you in my life again," Lucy said.

A yelp escaped before Belinda could cover her mouth with her hand.

"What? What is it, Bel?"

Belinda shook her head and stomped her foot.

"It's not fair. I'd change it if I could."

"Change what?"

"I'm graduating today."

Lucy felt like she was seeing life through a pinhole camera. Belinda's voice became softer and softer. Her words had less impact, they were temporary distractions from the truth of how alone Lucy was. When the two of them parted, it was with forced casualness, because the real feelings were too tough. Belinda gave Lucy what food she could get from the library and some valuable items she had in her locker. Then, she hugged Lucy good-bye like it wasn't a big deal. Neither of them could handle how big a deal it really was.

"Everything will be okay, Lucy. I won't abandon you. I'll get help."

Lucy shook her head as Belinda walked away. *Don't say that.* That was what Will said. That was exactly what Will had said. And he never came. Lucy became certain, as Belinda walked away, that she would do the same. Lucy wandered the halls in a daze, holding her belly, and telling herself that she would get through this, and maybe she would graduate before she gave birth, like Maxine, and then maybe the baby wouldn't die when it breathed its first breath of infected air. If she made it out, there could be a happy life for her out there, as a mother. Maybe with Will.

Before she knew it she'd come to a trashed stairwell in the ruins. The destruction and decay matched her mood. The walls were in terrible shape, full of cracks and holes. The first three stairs down from the landing were intact, but beyond that, they were gone. She stood at the edge of the landing and stared down. Fifteen feet below her was an uneven floor full of trash and beer cans. It reminded her of the remnants of a homeless man's bender that she had discovered once with her cousin. She'd found it gross and scary to look at back then, to imagine how sad the man must have been to spend the nights alone, drinking cheap liquor in a moldy heap of a building. Now she understood. She could see herself doing the same.

The rest of that man's life had probably been really sad, but the little booze party he had given himself hadn't been. She bet it had been the only peace he knew.

Lucy didn't even realize there was someone behind her. She hadn't noticed that she'd been followed ever since she walked away from her fatty friend. Stupid bitch. Might as well have been blind on top of being ugly. But Hilary had to give it to her on the disguise. If she hadn't spied Lucy taking all that crap out of her face, she would have missed this opportunity.

Hilary tightened her grip on the gun and slunk toward Lucy. She stepped softly, making sure to place each foot down where the floor was clean of any debris that might make noise under her shoes. She was only a few feet away now.

She leveled the gun's barrel at the back of Lucy's head as she crept. There was only one question on her mind. Should she waste a bullet on Lucy? They were so precious. They were the real source of her power.

Hilary remembered her tooth flushing down the toilet, and her trigger finger twitched. Her perfect tooth. The one that was meant to be in her mouth, that had fit better than this Freak girl's tooth ever would. Lucy had sent her pretty white tooth on a waterslide into a tank full of shit.

She was so close that the gun nearly tickled by Lucy's hair.

Hilary's shoe made the slightest squeak against the floor. Lucy whipped around, and Hilary shoved instead of shot. The shove tipped Lucy over the edge before she could see who'd shoved her. When Lucy realized she was falling, she screamed. She plummeted off the remains of the staircase, and thumped down to the floor below. Hilary peered over the edge and saw Lucy splayed out on the floor, still as a stone.

She had been fantasizing about this. It was why she always kept a pair of pliers in her purse. She still wanted Lucy's teeth. All of them. She craved them. She wanted to see Lucy walk the school with just pink gums smacking together, dripping with spit. She wouldn't be able to make *F* sounds and she'd sound like an idiot. And the best part of all—Lucy would never turn a boy's head again. Or maybe she would from time to time. But then, she'd smile, and the boys would run away in disgust.

Hilary was kicked out of her fantasy when the most atrocious-looking boy she'd ever seen emerged from the shadows near Lucy. His complexion was bloodless, his cheeks sunken, and he had broad, sharp shoulders. No fat left on his body, just ropes of twitching muscle underneath dry, shrink-wrapped skin. His lip was split, but the wet pink wound wasn't bleeding, and he didn't seem to notice. His eyes were cloudy and looked dumb, like farm-animal dumb. His hair was roughly cut off, in uneven lengths, like scissors had been held close to his scalp. In some scabby patches it looked like the hair had been pulled out at the roots. He wore a soiled dress tucked into black jeans that had developed a waxy sheen of burnished filth on the thighs.

The ghoulish boy grabbed Lucy's ankles and dragged her toward a dark hole in the wall.

No! Hilary thought.

She ran to the nearest intact stairwell, leapt down the stairs, and dashed back to the spot where Lucy had landed. She searched for the pair in a frenzy, and got so angry she nearly emptied her gun into the wall, but it would have done no good. They were gone.

WILL SLAMMED THE REAR DOOR OF GONZALO'S

custom minivan. The protective, steel blinds that crossed the
rear window rattled. There was nothing left to pack. They'd
gotten the list of supplies from Sam's dad that they should
look for on the way. They'd said their good-byes to the parents, and Will had a pocket full of good-luck charms after all
the hugs and handshakes. A silver dollar. A St. Christopher's
medal. A green rabbit's foot. An Indian head nickel. So much
hope was riding on them, and they were as ready as they'd
ever be to head out into the infected zone in search of the
cure. Gonzalo had given them his van. He'd said they'd need
it if they were going to make it to Minnesota. He wasn't coming with them. The big guy had departed the day before in a
jacked-up pickup truck to continue on his quest.

Will hoped Gonzalo would find Sasha out there. The world
would be too cruel if he didn't. Will looked to McKinley. Dark

gray, muscular clouds crashed together in slow motion above the school. He needed to find David. They had to get on the road before that storm caught up with them.

He moved his blistered hands across the short bristle of his freshly shorn head. He liked the springy touch to it, but he missed his white hair. He'd gotten so used to it, it had become a part of who he was. Still, he understood David's point, that on the road it would cause more trouble than it was worth. He looked to the plump veins spiderwebbing across his forearm and the clear separation between the different cords of muscles. This past month of manual labor and regular meals had packed meat onto his bones. He was stronger, quicker. More of a man.

Lucy would dig it.

Will and David had a long journey ahead of them, and even when they got to Minnesota, he recognized that there was no guarantee that there would be a cure waiting for them, nicely packaged in a single glossy pill. He knew things never went that perfectly. Yet, that didn't stop him from dreaming that it could go exactly that way, and that when they returned to McKinley in a week or so, Lucy could be in his arms again, uninfected, and they could finish that kiss. The one they'd been so close to having before the crane had pulled him up out of the quad.

It felt wrong to be apart from her, wrong at a core level. This couldn't be how other people felt when they were separated from someone they loved. There was no way. How could the world go on? He didn't feel like he was missing his high school sweetheart, he felt like he was missing his pancreas. The only way to feel better was to do something about it. It was why he'd pushed David so hard to go on the hunt for the cure.

"David?" Will called out.

Will walked around the section of fenced-in trailers, where graduates were stashed after being pulled out of the school. There were five trailers, including the one where Will had phased out of infection, each surrounded by a separate chain-link fence. Inside the second trailer's fence stood David. Will slowed. What was he doing there? He had said he was just going for a piss and then they would head out.

Will studied David's face. He wore a toothy smile. Wide and expectant, like a kid at a window waiting for his grandparents to pull into the driveway with a trunkful of toys.

Will's heart began to thump just like it did every time he saw the crane cable retract from dangling over the quad. There was always the hope that a new graduate would be hanging from its end. Someone with news about Lucy, or best of all— Lucy herself. But in the time since he'd been on the farm, no one else had graduated.

Will ran to the fence, his fingers wrapped through the chain links.

"Did they pull somebody out?" Will called out.

David didn't break his stare at the trailer door. "Last night. We were asleep. I just found out."

Will looked to the door. He could feel his face stretching into the same hopeful shape as David's.

"Who's in there?" Will said.

The possibility that Lucy could be in that trailer threatened to cleave Will's skull in two.

The door opened, and Belinda walked out. The basket of curly fries she called hair was still black, like a Nerd's, but soon her natural hair color, whatever that was, would overtake it. McKinley would get foggy in her mind just like it was in Will's. He had to talk to her.

He waved to her, but her eyes focused on David first. She stumbled back in shock, and the parent behind her, who'd tested her for the last traces of the virus, steadied her. David hurried to help, but Will was stuck on the other side of the fence. He watched as they guided Belinda to the gate. Belinda stared at David, her mouth agape and speechless as she walked.

It was odd for Will to watch someone else go through the same brain-flattening realization that he'd had that night in the rain. He knew how much Belinda had looked up to David. He knew how much she loved him. She'd been one of the original group of Scraps who had approached David about starting a gang. She had helped carry David to safety after he had been hanged. She had mourned his loss. Will had a clear memory of Belinda sobbing by the fire the night the remaining Loners had found out that David had died. He'd always felt closer to Belinda after that, but he'd never told her, and for some reason he knew he never would.

When Will reached the gate, the man who'd tested Belinda walked on and left David to lock up. By now, Belinda seemed to be able to stand on her own two feet.

"No—but—but David, how . . . ?" she managed to say as she neared him. She was crying, tears traveling down her round face like longitude lines on a globe.

"Long story," David said.

She nearly toppled David with the force of her hug. She squeezed him with all her might, and pancaked her cheek into his chest. She smiled with her eyes clamped shut. You would have thought she'd just found out Santa was real.

"I can't believe it," she whispered. "I can't believe it."

When she let go, David guided her toward the newly built bunkhouse.

"Come with us," he said, and for the first time, Belinda glanced over at Will.

"Hi," Will said.

She didn't reply, she simply walked with David. Will assumed that maybe she was still too caught up in the magic of David's existence. He walked in silence as Belinda and David talked. Belinda never acknowledged him once, and he began to wonder if she had a reason to snub him. What did she know?

There were too many information bombs that Will had yet to disarm before his brother could find them out, and now he was afraid of them all exploding at once. The history of McKinley that David knew had been abridged by Will. David knew that Will had fallen in with the Saints because the Loners had fallen apart, something that had been beyond Will's control. He knew Lucy had gone Sluts, but Will told him that he had lost contact with her at that point. He didn't tell him that they had fallen in love or that they had slept together. He and his brother were getting along for once, and it was too nice to mess up. Will didn't know what David still felt for Lucy, and he didn't want to know. And David seemed just as happy to avoid the subject entirely.

But as David and Will approached the bunkhouse, Belinda's presence made the topic of Lucy feel unavoidable. Will started to sweat. He couldn't take it anymore.

"How is she?" Will asked. "Lucy."

Belinda met Will's eyes for the first time. They were angry.

"Oh, you care?" she said.

David paused as he opened the bunkhouse door. He gave Belinda a curious look.

"Of course I care," Will said. "What do you mean?"

Her next words sucked all the air out of Will's world.

"She's pregnant."

"What?" David said.

Will's hearing went away. He saw David gesturing, but he

stopped processing the words that came out of his mouth. David waved Belinda inside. Will followed in a daze. Lucy was pregnant. Will shook his head. He dropped onto a cot. His hearing tuned back in with David's next three words: "Who's the father?"

Will's eyes snapped to Belinda. They screamed at her to not say if she knew. She looked away from Will, back to David, but she didn't answer him. Will could see her wrestling with a decision. She frowned and huffed air out her nose.

"She didn't say. She only told me right before I left."

David raked his fingers through his brown hair. He stumbled a little bit and sat down on a cot.

"Is she okay?" Will asked. He felt like an idiot asking it. What girl was ever okay being pregnant inside McKinley? He knew what it meant. And he got the answer he dreaded most.

"No," Belinda said. "She isn't."

David pounded a cot-side table with one heavy fist. He pounded the table four or five more times before grasping his forehead. They all sat in silence for a moment.

"I want to know everything," David said, his voice barely a whisper.

Belinda took a breath and told them the terrible story.

Will and David left Belinda behind in the bunkhouse. A parent would be along soon to educate her about her options going forward if she wanted to stay on the farm or leave in search of her family. She'd choose family. They all did.

Family. The idea meant something new to Will now, and he felt like he was going to be crushed under its weight.

"We have to do something," Will said as they walked toward the minivan.

"I know," David said.

Will waited a moment for more, but more didn't come.

"We have to go in," Will said.

"Don't be ridiculous."

"You heard what Belinda said. She's all alone."

David looked around as they walked, as if he was sure someone was eavesdropping. The only ears nearby belonged to the sheep.

"We have a plan, Will. Let's get the cure. We'll be back in a week. That'll fix everything."

"What if the cure's not real?"

"Don't say that."

"Why not? Because it might be true?"

"You're the one who was so convinced we needed to go in the first place. Now you're telling me you don't believe in it?"

"All I know is Lucy's pregnant. That's a fact. If we waste a week or two on this trip and come back with nothing, that's forever that Lucy's in there alone with no help. Anything could happen to her."

David fell back against the minivan and let out a groan.

"David, don't tell me you forgot what it feels like to be

in there. To not belong to a gang. To have no one watching your back. Can you even imagine facing all that while being pregnant?"

David faltered. "Jesus Christ."

"She needs us. We have to get her out. We have gas masks. They filter out the virus, right?"

"It's too dangerous. We'll make an announcement, have her come to the quad."

"We can't single her out. She'll be as bad off as Sam was. Someone will use her against us. Just like before."

"What about the guy who knocked her up?" David said with a splash of anger in his voice. "Huh? Isn't he looking after her?"

Will couldn't fathom a way to answer that.

"What if he's not?" Will finally said. "What if he's just some dickhead that doesn't care what happens to her?"

It didn't inspire the response Will was looking for. David began to sneer. With his black eye patch, he looked almost frightening.

"Do you know who she was dating before you left?"

Will shook his head before he could say something. "I don't—I don't think so."

"No idea?"

"I don't know, maybe some Nerd with stupid hair," Will said. "I saw her with him at this party, but he looked like a big pussy. We can't count on him."

David stared at the school. Will understood that going into the school was madness, but Lucy needed them. He stared at David and waited. If anything would bring him back to his old self, it would be Lucy in trouble.

Finally, David shook his head.

"There's no way."

"But—"

"It's a death sentence," David said. He was raising his voice, trying to drown Will out. Will hated that.

"And what if the cure isn't a rumor?" David continued. "Then, we would've gotten ourselves killed when there was an easy answer. And Lucy would still be in danger."

"You don't get it," Will said. Not that he could unless Will told him the truth. But he knew that would only make his brother angrier, and then Will would be on the defensive.

"No, you don't get it," David said. "You didn't go on pointless missions to get your old pal Gates's bullshit, and watch good people cough up their lungs and die, because some angry kids wanted revenge. You're not infected anymore, Will. You don't realize how afraid you should be of everyone in that school."

Will stared at David, wondering how long his brother had been judging him for what he'd done with the Saints inside. He wondered how long David had watched him from above and done nothing to help.

"At least I know how to do the right thing even when I'm

scared," Will said. "Which is something you must'a forgotten."

"Fuck you."

"No, fuck you," Will said and turned. He stomped away from the minivan. The distant rumble of thunder echoed the snort of pigs nearby. Will looked up. The clouds above were darker and more knotted than before.

He didn't know where he was going, but he wanted to get away from David before he said something worse. They should've been on the road by now, but the idea of spending days in the van with David seemed impossible. Each scrape of his shoes through the grass was loud. There was another crack of thunder, and with it the truth of his situation fully sank in for the first time.

". . . holy shit," Will muttered, his eyes wandering as his mind reeled.

He was going to be a father.

He felt dizzy. The sky swirled. The distant mountain range looked like a row of dog teeth. That was where Gonzalo was headed, into the Rockies, in search of Sasha. His love for her was relentless. Nothing could stop him from holding her again.

Will breathed deep. The air was crisp and fragrant, and Will wanted to remember how it smelled. He wanted to remember every detail of what it felt like out here.

He was going back in.

9

THE STORM HAD PULLED ITS CLOAK OVER the farm. It was almost eight o'clock. The sun had sunk, and the winds had risen. David walked the pasture fence, and swept the campus with a flashlight.

"Will!" he called out, but his voice was whisked away by a sudden gust. The steady rumble of wind was the only response.

Will had gone missing, and David couldn't convince anyone that it was worth worrying about. All the parents were too busy rushing to prep for the storm, getting animals and equipment under cover and battening down every hatch. David tried to stay calm by convincing himself Will had gotten swept up in helping. But given their argument, that didn't sound like Will. David cursed himself. He should've kept his mouth shut, but his brother had always been an expert at driving him crazy. It was as if Will was allergic to rational thought.

"Come on . . . ," he said to himself.

David hated being out after sunset. It reminded him just how blind he was. Darkness wrapped around his field of vision and squeezed. His Cyclops sight forced him to scan his surroundings like a security camera. In his travels through the infected zone, he'd trained himself to be a creature of the day because night felt as vast as the ocean. In the dark, everything had the drop on him.

He'd never gotten over being mauled by Hilary. She'd taken a piece of him when she'd taken his eye. It had been Lucy who'd helped him feel like a human being again. He'd never forget that. Not that it mattered. She'd already forgotten him. She'd had to, he supposed. He was a ghost as far as McKinley was concerned. Life in there had gone on without him. And it hurt. Far worse than he'd ever imagined it would. He felt like an idiot, thinking of her as this angel who'd nursed him back to health. Lucy had someone else's baby inside her. She was forever connected to whoever that was. She probably didn't even think about David.

A gust assaulted him, and for a moment the pressure of the wind felt more real than the ground underneath his feet. His jean jacket had a sheepskin lining but even so, the cold wind slithered in through the neck, through the wrist holes, between the buttons, up his back, and threatened to make the light perspiration on his skin frost over.

"Will!" he shouted again, passing his flashlight beam

across the wheat field. The wheat whipped in a panic.

Will didn't understand how afraid he should be of McKinley. Out in the infected zone it was open space. At least there you could run away. In McKinley they'd be trapped. Completely at the mercy of the infected. Maybe if he'd told Will exactly what he'd seen out there, he'd get it. But David had never found the strength to talk about it, let alone think about it.

He could still hear the screaming.

Once Will had been identified by Sam and the parents as Gates's right-hand man, things had gotten tense for David on the farm. He'd had to go the extra mile on everything to prove his loyalty, especially when it came to delivering on Gates's demands. When the Saints leader had pushed Sam's dad's limits and requested a pool for the quad, David had put himself first in line to retrieve it. He and two other parents traveled forty miles to the Pool Liquidators in Bristol. There was trouble along the way, but nothing like they found at the store. When they'd discovered an aboveground pool in the parking lot filled with a red stew of blood and bodies of hunters, it was already too late. They should have turned around when they saw the buzzards overhead. Instead, they'd been surrounded by a ragged crew of infected. There were eleven of them, more boys than girls, none of them over thirteen years old, the youngest infected David had ever seen, but by far the most frightening. They had attacked like a pack of coyotes. All eleven had rushed Deb Winchester, a proud mother of three with the most boisterous, wonderful laugh David had ever heard. The pack had climbed on her and had crushed her down to the ground in seconds. They had torn off her mask, and her frantic screams had become a low roar as lung sludge had erupted from her mouth.

David dug his hands down into his jacket pockets and turned to head back to the minivan. The wind surged. A speck of something hit David in the eye and he stopped dead in his tracks. He rubbed, frantically. It was only a fleck of dirt or hay, but anything getting in that eye turned him to jelly. When he had nightmares now, they were black.

Rain began to fall and created a thick wall of sound. It pelted his face, forcing him to squint his one good eye. David slowed his search. Will would come back to the minivan eventually. Then, they could go. This was wasted energy.

David heard an odd noise on his blind side. A clap of metal on metal. He listened for it again but heard only the huff of the wind and the rhythm of rain. *Clap.* There it was again. *Clap-clap.* David's eye followed his flashlight beam. The sound didn't match anything he knew on the farm. It came at random, a few claps in a row, then nothing, then one, and on and on, like a blind kid trying to play with a paddleball.

He went toward the sound, and his flashlight guided him to the crane. The base of it was a vehicle the size of a Greyhound bus, and four massive arms stretched out, planting it in the ground to give it a wider base. At the rear of the vehicle was the operating booth for the crane arm itself.

Clap-clap. The door to the booth was wide open, flapping in the wind.

David quickened his pace. Something wasn't right. The crane was always locked up at night. David stepped on something hard; it tripped him up. He looked down. A crowbar in the grass.

He clambered up the short ladder into the operating booth. He dropped into the plush orange seat. The control board arced and filled the dash in front of him, below the wrap-around windshield. His seat rumbled underneath him. The motor was still on.

David hadn't heard its chugging over the sound of the wind and pelting rain until he'd gotten close. He prayed for some sensible explanation for this. He looked at the wall behind the operator's seat, where the crane operator's gas mask hung. It was gone.

David looked up through the broad windshield and up the tall crane arm that extended up into the sky. Someone was climbing the crane arm and they were almost to the tip. David burst out of the booth and strained to get a better look. He saw the person wore a gas mask and a backpack. He saw he was male.

He saw it was Will.

"Stop!" David screamed up. Rain peppered his mouth. Will didn't hear, or he didn't want to listen. Will lowered himself onto the metal cable that hung from the crane, and he zipped down it, past the roofline, to where David couldn't see, but he knew where he was going. The crane's tip was over the quad.

David's heart punched at his ribs. Will didn't just do that. David's world caved in on him. How could Will be so stupid? He waited for the parents on watch to sound an alarm. There was only howling wind and slapping rain. How could Will go in with only a gas mask to . . .

Oh dear God.

He knew which gas mask Will was wearing, the one from the crane. David had worn it too. That mask had seen heavy use, and the filter hadn't been replaced in a while. A fresh filter was guaranteed for forty-eight hours of continuous use. After that, you were pushing your luck.

Will's filter might not last him until morning.

David cursed Will with every foul word he could think of because it was the only resistance he could summon. His feet were already moving. He'd already turned off the crane's motor so that no one would hear. He'd already grabbed a gas mask with a fresh filter for himself from the van, and was shoving other essentials into a backpack. A fresh filter for Will and the crane remote. It was big and orange, and it could move the arm and lower and raise the cable. He'd use it to pull them back out. He stuffed in a hatchet and an energy bar that he had no idea how he'd eat with a mask on his head.

He was wasting time. Will was getting farther into the

school by the second. The longer David took, the harder it would be to find him and replace his filter. The more infected he might run into. He wanted this over within ten minutes, in and out.

"I'm gonna kill him," he said.

He stood at the base of the crane arm, staring up the long crane arm as it disappeared into the sky. The sky had darkened since he'd gathered his supplies and now the charcoal clouds began to churn. He couldn't see the tip of the boxy crane arm anymore. The arm just got thinner as it got higher until it seemed to disappear. Another gust blew David's hair to the side. He heard the stray dogs outside the farm moan in sympathy with the wind.

One foot in front of the other. He moved his arms and legs mechanically, like they were pistons with set paths. He kept his eye focused on each steel cross brace as he grabbed ahold of them. The wind blew the heat right out of his fingers. When David reached the halfway mark of his climb, he could feel the crane's sway. One misplaced hand, one lean too far to counter the wind, and he'd take a fall that would end him. He looked up the arm. The zigzag ladder ahead looked like nightmare train tracks extending into the clouds. The wind lashed out at him. He hugged close to the crane, wanting to catch as little wind as possible. He looked at the ground and his stomach bobbed up and down like it was suspended from rubber bands. David knew he couldn't rest too long or the idea of quitting would needle into his brain and slowly leach away his resolve. He took a breath and kept climbing. He refused to look down until, finally, he was there, at the top.

David crooked his elbow around one of the cross braces, and unzipped his bag enough to pull the gas mask out of it. He squeezed it over his head and his first inhale felt like he was sipping peanut butter through a straw. He realized that he had no idea when he would be taking this mask off again. He was locking his head into a jail cell. He lingered there at the peak, trying to regulate his breath, feeling the pull of the filter, like he was at the foothills of emphysema.

The quad waited for him below. The dirt scarred from countless battles. The quad looked almost foreign from this vantage point. The days when he'd fought for food on that gouged dirt down there seemed deep in the past. David made the transition to the cable. A hundred feet of steel wobbled in slow motion between his legs. There was no going back now.

David slid down the line in short bursts, never letting himself drop more than three feet before clamping his legs and fists tight again. The cable swung and twisted in the wind. Rain slapped his face. Near the bottom, he let his grip go loose, and he zipped down the cable, certain that he was making the worst decision of his short life.

David's feet hit the quad.

He pissed a little bit. He was sure he could feel the virus all around him, coating the skin of his neck and wrists. Fear crushed in on him. David's breathing went hyperactive. He sucked in breaths harder than the mask would allow. His stomach vacuumed.

David forced himself to relax. Gradually, as he began to draw in longer breaths, the air came easier, and his heart quit having a fit.

He headed for the elevator.

10

THE FIRST THING LUCY WAS AWARE OF WAS
pain. Blades of it, skewering her through her side. Then more
pain. Stings and aches all over her front. She was lying on
a rough, uneven surface. The air smelled like gasoline and
feces.

Lucy popped her eyes open and saw that she was in the
corner of a room full of rubble, where water streamed down
the cracked walls and dripped from the sagging ceiling. She
lay on a pile of book bags.

There were other people in the room with her. Burnouts.
A boy with long white hair that hung in front of his face sat
crumpled against the wall, seemingly unconscious, with a
damp piece of yellowed cloth in his limp hand. A lanky girl,
with long stretched-out legs and a nose like a beak, lay on
his lap, eyes half closed, drool spilling off her lower lip, with
her hand down the front of her unbuttoned pants. A boy, with

shiny burn scars where most of his scalp should have been, was splayed out on the floor, hand down his sweatpants, masturbating to the sight of the passed-out, tall girl. Lucy jerked her gaze elsewhere.

In another corner, a boy in a Santa hat pissed into a wide-mouth plastic water jug full of shit. He was standing like Godzilla amid a city of other water bottles on the floor, all half full with a brown soup of urine and feces. Each bottle had a latex glove rubber banded to the mouth. Some of the gloves were empty and limp, but most were in various degrees of inflation. There were other kids in the room too, mostly passed out. Dead, sunken eyes in ghastly faces. Greasy snarls of gray hair. Unwashed skin. Stringy muscles stretched over their bones.

They all looked hungry. Especially the three that Lucy had suddenly realized were eyeing her. Two boys and a girl. The bigger boy wore a dead teacher's suit. The smaller boy wore only sneakers, black gloves, and white briefs that were gray with filth. The girl had dreads. All three were getting to their feet. They walked toward her.

Lucy tried to stand up and she got dizzy. Pressure pounded in her head and she had to lean against the wall to not fall over. The big guy in the dead teacher's suit motioned to the other two, and they each ran to a doorway. They were blocking the exits. The boy in his underwear twitched as he clapped his hands together in quick, joyous little bursts.

The girl spun in a circle and choked herself with both hands.

Lucy tried to call out to the big one in the suit as he walked toward her. *No!* she wanted to scream, but her voice was only a rasp. He mimicked her, his white gumball eyes blasting open as he yawned a silent scream. Branched veins pulsed in his neck and down his forehead. His movements were slow, but his whole body shook with tension. Lucy hurt, her stomach, her hips, her chest, her face, and her soul. She knew she didn't have enough strength to contend with him.

She pushed off the wall and tried to slip past him, but something jerked on her ankle and stopped her short. She looked down to find a black nylon cord tied tightly to her ankle. The cord's other end extended through a hole in the wall and knotted around a plumbing pipe. Next to the hole, a piece of toilet paper was stuck to the wall, and written on it in the worst handwriting Lucy had ever seen were the words *Be Back Soon.* There was a lopsided heart drawn next to the message.

Lucy whipped her head back to see the suit still stomping toward her. She formed her fingers into claws and raised them up, ready to plunge them into his eyes.

A boy wearing a dress over jeans ran into the room, past the girl in the doorway, and shoved the boy in the suit to the ground.

"Stay away from my stuff!" the boy in the dress screamed down at him.

The boy in the suit scurried back, holding his shoulder and grumbling. The boy in the dress turned to Lucy and came walking over. Again, she was sure she was going to die, until he walked past her and picked up a plastic V8 bottle that was one-third full of yellowish liquid. He shook it over his head and bellowed at the others, "Mine!"

When he seemed satisfied that the others weren't going to try and steal his bottle anymore, the boy in the dress calmed down. He knelt down at Lucy's side with an entirely different energy. His eyes looked worried, and his movements were gentle.

His dress was a satiny slip that once could've been a light lilac, but now was blackened like a mechanic's rag. One of the straps was broken and that side hung down, exposing his tiny dark nipple. He had a frame as skinny as a shaved rabbit's, and his skin was covered in red rashes.

He tried to touch her knee and she jerked away. He frowned a little and pulled a sharpened letter opener out of his pocket. Lucy formed her fingers into claws again. The boy cut the cord around her ankle and put the blade away, setting her free. As he was leaning forward to do it, a glittering gold necklace swung forward that hung around his neck.

Her necklace.

She remembered him. This was the boy from the ruins who had tried to steal her necklace when the Loners were smuggling David out of the school. The chemical-huffing boy who'd said the necklace had belonged to his mother. The broken boy who had confessed that he had escaped the lab that had created the virus, and then tried to hide from the military in this school. The boy who had infected them all.

"Dey scare you?" he said. His voice was scratchy and full of hiss like an old record, his vowels elongated by a strong Southern drawl. "Real sorry 'bout them."

Lucy stared at the necklace at rest on his pale flesh. It had been a token of Will's love for her. She was sorry she'd ever let it go, but it didn't matter now. What she needed to do was get out of here.

"I have to go," she croaked, and tucked her legs underneath her to stand. Just the intention to move hurt.

He nodded. "Back to your plant room?"

Lucy stared at the boy. The room felt colder and smaller, and he seemed bigger, more dangerous than ever. She swallowed to wet the gravel in her throat.

"What plant room?"

He smiled and revealed a set of teeth like a crumbling housing project.

"Where you live, silly."

"How do you . . ."

"I watch you."

Lucy backed up.

"What do you mean, 'you watch me'?" she said.

He waved his hands back and forth. "Don't be scared. Hold on. Just wait here a second. Don't leave."

The boy bounded out of the room. Lucy looked around. The Burnout in his underwear had walked away from the other doorway. He was slapping the wall with a heavy metal chain and laughing. The one in the suit was making out with the dread-headed girl. If Lucy was going to run, it had to be now. She pressed her back against the corner of the room and pushed up with her legs. Every inch up brought a new level of pain until she had to stop. Her knees bent inward and knocking, her arms splayed and hunting for some crack to hold on to.

The boy in the dress ran back into the room, and Lucy sunk back down with a sob. He had her scuffed garbage bag in one hand, and Minnie, the hydrangea flower, in the other. The boy sat at the foot of Lucy's backpack-pile bed. He plopped the garbage bag down between his legs and proceeded to pull out all her stuff.

"You don't have to leave," he said with that same big, rotten smile. "I fetched all your things, see?"

Lucy stared at her pathetic pile of things and how the boy was touching them.

"It ain't safe for you out there," he went on.

"I can take care of myself," Lucy mustered.

He nodded as if he agreed with her completely. "You're all fucked up though. From your fall."

Fall. Lucy remembered looking down on that pit of trash. Then, a shove and the panic of having nothing under her. Someone had pushed her.

"You," Lucy said. "Why did you push me?"

The boy shook his head. "No, no. Not me. I'd never. You must'a slipped or somethin'. I'd never."

She wondered if he'd done anything to her while she was asleep.

"How you gonna get food all fucked up?"

"I—"

He slapped his bony chest. "I can feed you. You're safe here."

She wanted to say no, but at that moment she realized with great clarity how much she craved to be taken care of.

"Why would you want to do that?" she said.

His voice rose slightly. "You gave me back my momma's necklace." He clutched the pendant at the end of the necklace. "You're a good person. I want to be your friend."

She could see ghosts in his eyes. She could see the weight of everything he was responsible for and how he was being crushed underneath it every second. She could see why he huffed himself into a stupor every day. She wouldn't want to be him either.

From out of his own sack he took a can of tuna, a can opener, and a set of plastic silverware in a cellophane bag. He opened the can and handed it up to her.

"You should eat. And rest. You took a bad fall."

She wanted to rest. She wanted to lie down for a month. The tin of tuna in her hand made her belly rumble. Lucy began to wonder if that was more than a craving, if it wasn't the baby, as tiny as it had to be, crying out to her, telling her it needed food. Lucy's free hand moved to her belly, and she felt a rushing sense of relief that it was the one place on her body where there was no pain. Only warmth. And she began to cry.

"I'm sorry," she whispered.

"Naw, I'm sorry. I'm sorry," he said. He began to mutter it.

She didn't know what he was talking about. She wasn't talking to him. She was talking to her child. Her baby was okay. She couldn't explain it; she just knew it with total certainty. This baby inside her was the one good thing she had left, and she would do whatever it took to stay alive.

Lucy ate. The pleasure in her mouth and stomach numbed the pain elsewhere, and her brain began to work a little better. She took in the room, the boy, and the Burnouts with a new frame of mind. Maybe she could milk some more food out of the kid. As long as he was around, the others seemed content to lay off. Even if she got out of the ruins, this boy knew where she lived. She'd have to find somewhere new. She could stay in David and Will's old elevator home for a while, but how long could she keep making that jump from the top of the elevator to the maintenance ladder without putting the baby at risk? She didn't even want to do it once.

The boy took his jug of yellowness that he'd protected so fiercely before and dribbled some of the liquid into a rag. He covered his nose and mouth with the damp cloth and took a deep inhale. His eyes unfocused. His hand dropped and the rag tumbled out of it. The tension in his face and in his muscles melted away. His fidgeting stopped, and his mouth drifted open. There was a vacancy on his face, like all brain activity had stopped.

After a little while he drifted back to reality and snuck a glance at her.

"So what, you sit around and sniff glue all day?" Lucy said through a tuna-clogged mouth.

He laughed. It made his teeth stick out. He reached for his jug and tried to pat it, but missed. His dreamy smile faded and his face grew gravely serious.

"Naw, the glue's all gone," he said. "The chemicals from the science labs are gone. Most of the markers are dried out." There was sorrow in his voice, like these were tragic facts. "Every once in a blue moon you'll find a can of hair spray, or roach killer, that some kid asked the parents for, some aerosol somethin', but those are getting real tough to find now." He brightened. "Never figured I'd have gasoline though. Like it was sent from God up in heaven."

"Where'd you get it?"

"That motorcycle. Boy, that sucker was loud, wadn't it? I hunted it down to the quad. When I got there, dat fuckin'-sorry, dat Gates kid, he was dead when I got there, and the bike was still runnin', and I seen you, in the distance, stumblin' into one of the halls. I had a tube and I siphoned that gas real quick, 'fore anyone else come. I can still taste it."

The boy turned to Lucy with big, hazy eyes.

"I followed you home," he said, his voice lilting and far away. "Didn't want nothing more to happen to you. You're so good."

Lucy looked down. How long had he been trying to protect her from the shadows? It freaked her out.

The boy managed to get his fingers around the jug handle and he shook it. The gas sloshed against the plastic.

"Gotta make this last, or it's back to stinkers," he said.

"What are stinkers?" Lucy was scared to know.

The boy pointed to the bottles of sewage with the rubber gloves on top.

"That's a drug?" Lucy said, aghast.

He nodded. "They get stashed on windowsills in the quad. Sun cooks the crap up inside and all them fumes make the gloves puff out."

Lucy looked at the bottles in disbelief.

"I never tasted nothing worse in my life, but one suck offa that glove, and whoo . . . you go someplace else, boy. You see people too."

"That's disgusting."

The smile faded from his face.

"I know, but . . . it's worth it sometimes," he said. He looked at her with clearer eyes than before. "It's the only way I get to talk to Momma."

Lucy put the empty tuna can on the ground, and touched her belly with both hands.

"I'm going," she said. She didn't have to wait this decision out. The baby told her what to do.

The boy struggled to pull himself up and fought his gasoline high with a couple of slaps to his head. Lucy leaned forward and pushed all her belongings and the hydrangea back into the garbage bag.

"You sure?" he said. His face was in a panic.

Lucy felt a chill wash through her. Would he try to stop her? The pain she felt standing up was obstacle enough.

"Yeah," Lucy said.

She shuffled past him, toward one of the crumbling door-ways. With each step, she prayed that her rejection wouldn't cause him to flip out. Would he get mean and sic the others on her? Would he come up from behind and snake his ropy arms around her neck? She could imagine the dirty satin of his slip rubbing against the back of her neck as he choked her unconscious and tied her up again.

Lucy reached the doorway and took a deep breath.

Cramps knifed her in the side again and she doubled over. The boy ran to her, but she pushed him back with a solid shove. She didn't look back, she lifted herself upright, and hobbled away from the room.

The fall into the trash had only made the old injuries from her battle with Gates worse. Her body hurt two times over. And her mind hurt from how many times the rug had been pulled out from under her. But her heart hurt most of all. She missed Will. She missed Belinda. She missed having friends. She missed David existing. The world had seemed brighter when he was alive.

She kept shuffling forward, even though she had no idea what her destination was. From back in the room, she heard the boy call out to her.

"I didn't tell you my name. They call me Bile."

She slogged into a sopping wet hall. He shouted one more thing, but it was very quiet because she had already traveled far.

"I'll always be here for you," he said.

11

SWEAT POOLED INSIDE DAVID'S MASK. IT
splashed up as he jogged down the hall, occasionally wetting
his lips. The mask was torturous. It itched anywhere the
rubber pressed against his skin. He was dying to dig a finger
under the lining and scratch, but that would have been the
last thing he ever did.

The virus was everywhere. He was wading through clouds
of invisible poison, and he couldn't help but feel that it had
a mind of its own, that it was searching for a loose seam to
slither through so it could swim down to the pink flesh of his
lungs and feast.

David had a hoodie on under his jacket, and the hood covered his gas mask and his face underneath it fairly well. As
long as no one looked too close. But if they did, and they saw
his eye patch, he had no idea what would happen. He used to
be famous here.

David slowed down because he was getting out of breath. It was just after midnight. He'd been in school for four hours and wasn't any closer to finding Will. The elevator had been a bust, no trace of Will. David had decided to head to the Stairs next, but he knew the chances of Will being there weren't great. There was a better chance that he and his brother would end up circling each other through the school until Will blew his lungs out onto his face shield. If he hadn't already. David shuddered at the thought of Will dying so brutally.

He heard a noise. He stopped.

He felt the floor rumble under his feet. Something was coming his way. Fast. David panicked. He ran to the nearest classroom. Locked. It was too late. In his periphery he saw someone come tearing around the corner. He looked. It wasn't a someone. It was a wild hog.

The snarling beast with protruding tusks charged him and he froze. Its heavy hooves cracked against the floor. White spit flung from its mouth. The beast bolted right past, and before David could even think to feel glad, seven shirtless Skaters, carrying sharpened broom handles, charged around the corner after the pig. David kept his head down and turned away. He hugged the lockers. They made pig squealing noises as they rushed past, and one of them laughed. When he dared to look up, he saw them disappear around another corner after the animal.

What had happened to this place?

McKinley was not how he remembered it. The building was in worse shape. Holes had been knocked through drywall, and entire sections of wall had been removed. Remaining walls were nearly blacked out with pen and marker graffiti. The floor was so dirty it was beginning to look like asphalt.

People were acting differently as well. They seemed more violent. He had already seen brutal altercations as he had snuck through the halls, hiding in one locker after another, darting from empty classrooms to maintenance closets. Through locker slats and from behind doors, he'd seen McKinley kids robbing each other at knifepoint. He'd watched as one Skater had been surrounded by three Geek girls. They'd told him to strip and give them his clothes or they'd beat him with hammers. He'd seen two Nerds trying to get a rolling book cart, stocked with water bottles, back to the library. A group of Saints had tackled them, repeatedly kicked them in the ribs, and dumped some of the bottles on their heads. The Saints left them on the ground, wet and writhing, and made off with the rest of the bottles. David had seen a frail Geek girl get felt up by Varsity boys as they were emptying her backpack onto the floor. Through all of it, David had stayed hidden and done nothing.

In the past, he would have done something about these situations, not watch them. He'd have intervened. But each time he watched one of these assaults go down, he'd only felt afraid for himself, that they would hear his breathing, that they'd tear his mask off, that he would die, and Will would too. He knew he had reason to be afraid, but David couldn't shake the feeling that he had changed, that he had lost some part of himself that was right, and true, and brave.

David picked up the pace, and reached the Stairs without any more animal attacks. He stood staring at the doorway of the old Loner base. The door had been removed. He knew there were no Loners inside. He knew that. But he didn't realize how hard it would be to see his old home abandoned. It hurt nearly as much as seeing his parents' house overrun with raccoons and squatters, and he'd lived in that place all his life. As he walked into the desolate armory, his mind leapt back to when this bottom landing had been heaped with weapons. He ascended the Stairs where his fellow Loners had once greeted him with smiles, grateful for the safe home and sense of family he'd provided. He was startled by the little moments, the forgettable exchanges, that crackled in his brain—a hidden smile from Dorothy, the twins feeding each other, Will actually reading, Sasha teasing Gonzalo about how she was going to cut his hair in his sleep, and the first time Lucy had laughed at one of David's jokes.

It almost made David smile.

Then, he saw the lounge wall. Light from the hall spotlighted a slew of profanity about the Loners, written in field paint. The sentiment was signed by Varsity. They'd enjoyed doing this, that much was clear. It made David bristle. He hurried across the empty landing and up the next flight. The Stairs were running out of dark corners where he might find Will, and it was making David anxious. But there was still his room, at the very top.

When David got there, he found his curtain entrance still hanging. He pushed one heavy flap aside, and saw a kid crouched in the corner with his back to David.

"Will?"

The kid turned and jumped to a fighting stance. He had blue hair. A Freak. He had a short two-by-four in his hand, ready to swing. His other hand was deformed, bent and twisted into a claw.

"Mort . . . ," David said.

Mort dropped the two-by-four and it clattered on the ground. He rushed to David and got his face right up against David's mask. Mort's eyes danced around David's face.

"You're alive!" Mort laughed high and loud. He did a little jig, hugged David, and wouldn't let go. "I'm so glad to see you."

"Okay, okay, Mort, take it easy," David said, but in truth, all the joy Mort was displaying warmed David. He'd remembered that his gang had loved him, but he'd forgotten how it felt.

Mort broke away.

"I wish you didn't have to see me with blue hair."

"Don't worry about it."

"Things just sort of fell apart," he went on. "I still come back here to think about old times."

David wanted to interrupt and change the subject to Will, but he was touched.

"Sometimes I'll run into Leonard or Ritchie here and they're doing the same thing."

"Really?" David said.

Mort nodded with a smile. "I wish things were like they used to be. I wish the Loners hadn't—"

"Me too."

Mort sighed.

"Mort, I really need your help."

Mort straightened. His eyes bloomed.

"Anything for you, David."

He said it like he was ready to receive orders, and David was still his leader, as if no time at all had passed.

"I need to find Will."

"Oh, I heard Will graduated."

David shook his head. "He came back into the school, and I have to find him or he's going to die. Can you think of any place he might be? Anywhere. He's looking for Lucy."

Mort snorted a laugh. "What, is she knocked up or something?"

"Yes. She is."

Mort's grin went flat. He broke eye contact with David.

"Why did you say that?" David said.

"Huh?" Mort said without looking up. "I don't know . . . good guess?"

"But why did you smile?"

"If I was Lucy, I'd hide somewhere no one goes. Maybe the dump?"

"Mort."

"Um." Mort drew circles on the floor with his toe. "I heard from a Slut that Lucy and Will dated. She liked him so much she got the Sluts in a huge brawl with the Saints to save him from Gates. This guy, Gates, was—"

"I know who Gates is," David mumbled, turning inward. Will and Lucy had dated. It stung him to hear, but he guessed it made sense. Will had always been in love with Lucy. David had died. They were a comfort to each other.

"I just—" David rasped. "He would have told me."

"You said he came back right after he heard Lucy was pregnant?"

The math clicked in David's brain. "That little motherfucker."

THE PORCELAIN TOILET LUCY SAT ON HAD
once been white, but was now gray and gouged with black
scratches. Its bowl was cracked and it leaked a thin dribble
of toilet water continuously, leaving the floor of the stall wet
and the air thick with the stink of mold. No one went to this
bathroom, it was too deep into the ruins, too far from anything most McKinley students cared about. Lucy'd had to
crawl underneath a collapsed doorway to even get into it.

Something was wrong.

Blood poured from her. Too much. More than any period
she'd ever had, and full of clumps and clots. It felt like a
river of warm caramel flowing out of her. She was shaking.
It had begun with the feeling that there was a Rubik's Cube
trying to solve itself inside her uterus, twisting and crank-
ing and scraping her with its sharp corners. The clenching
cramps hurt so bad she'd thought she'd been going into labor.

She'd told herself that was impossible. It was just her injuries from the fall, and that she only had to find somewhere to rest.

Something large fell out of her and plopped down into the water.

Lucy sat bolt upright at the noise. She didn't want to look. She looked at her pale, bruised knees. Her pulse thunked in her neck. She felt empty. She sat staring at the coat hook on the back of the stall door, the curve of chrome with a bulbous end, wishing she was somewhere else, somebody new, far away from here.

When Lucy rose to her feet, it was on baby deer legs. With her pants still around her ankles she turned to face the bowl of blood. She could feel more blood trailing down her thighs, but she didn't bother to wipe herself clean. It didn't matter that she was messy. What mattered was in the toilet.

Lucy began to sob as she reached her hands toward the red water. There were dark clots floating in the watery blood and little bits of pink tissue, and gray pieces too. One clot was larger than all the others. She reached in and picked it up. The water slipped through her fingers, leaving just a clump of red.

She couldn't breathe as she staggered out of the stall and over to the sink. She turned on the water and held the clump under the stream. As the blood washed away, she saw it was a clear sac, with something that looked like a piece of liver attached to it. What was inside the sac didn't look human, it looked like an alien shrimp with a big head and a curly tail. But it wasn't an alien. It was her baby.

Lucy screamed. She felt the floor strike her kneecaps. She felt herself pulling on her own hair. The world became a blur. The next thing she was aware of was running from the bathroom. Pounding her feet, pumping her arms. Nothing she could do, nothing she could think of, could make what she'd seen go away. There was nowhere to run. No place in the school would reverse what had just happened.

She wanted it to not be true.

She begged God to make it not be true.

The sadness crushed in on her from all sides.

She had to stop this feeling, she couldn't bear it.

She couldn't.

She saw the world through a dense cloud of smog. Her brain and her body felt a mile apart. Lucy didn't even remember deciding to go there, but before she knew it, she was shuffling back into the Burnout drug den. Dirty kids inhaling dirty air together to forget where or who they were. And for the first time, Lucy understood the faraway look in those dirty kids' eyes. They were gone completely. That was where Lucy wanted to be.

"Bile . . . ," she said.

When Bile saw her face he must have known, or maybe it was when he saw the blood seeping through the crotch of her pants, because he wrapped her in a bony, dry-skinned hug.

"My . . . my baby."

Those were the only words she could get out.

He squeezed her harder. He walked her across the room, stepping over kids who sat against the wall with their chins resting on their chests. They came to the water bottles of human waste with the inflated gloves coming off the top. Stinkers, he'd called them.

Bile reached down and picked up one. He twisted the base of the glove and held the twist of rubber to keep the gas in while he pulled the glove off the bottle. The scent of pungent sewage burned in Lucy's nostrils and she almost lost her nerve. He tied off the end of the glove like a balloon. Then he pinched the tip of the thumb and snipped the end with a pair of scissors.

He told her to put her mouth on it. She was afraid. She looked at him. He nodded with understanding eyes.

"You'll feel better," he said. "You won't feel nothing at all."

She realized that this was why she'd come here. And that was why she was so afraid. She wanted this. She looked at Bile in his soiled slip. He was staring at her with concern, like a worried school nurse.

"One big breath. Just do like this," he said and then mimicked sucking on his thumb.

She put her lips on the bitter rubber. He nodded and smiled at her, revealing the brown rot of his teeth. She bit the glove.

She thought of Will. And it cut her in two. Tears fell down her cheek. She was sorry. She was so sorry.

Your baby is dead.

Lucy let her teeth part, and inhaled. Bile squeezed the plump glove to make sure she got it all. The taste didn't hit her until she'd finished taking the breath in. The smell of shit was on her tongue. It was in her throat, in her lungs, and she wanted it out of her at once. Bile put his rough hand over her mouth and pinched her nose shut between his thumb and knuckle.

"You gotta hold it!"

She pried at his fingers, trying to get them off her as her lungs marinated in methane, and the taste sunk into her tongue. It was becoming part of her. She struggled but he was too strong. Her vision began to darken. Her lungs kicked. Her legs went soft.

He let go and she fell to the ground. The back of her head smacked against the wall but it didn't hurt. Nothing hurt anymore. She couldn't even feel her head. It had become a dandelion puffball, and a breeze scattered all her seeds into the air. She was everywhere at once, moving, traveling away, and soon the room, as she knew it, was a memory, even though she understood she was still in it. The filth, the garbage, the stinkers, the scabby kid in the back of the room who was defecating into a bucket that his friend had just pissed in—none of it meant a thing.

"Lucy."

She looked up. David was there. His white hair shined. He picked her up like he was carrying her over the threshold after their wedding. And then it was true, he was in a tux and she was in her mother's wedding dress. Her veil was over her face, and she wanted so badly to lift it and kiss him, but when she tried, she found that it was just too long. No matter how much fabric she tugged up over her head, there was always more, the veil was infinite.

She hugged his body and buried her face into the dry-cleaned fabric of his suit. She let her tears soak in. She could hear the heavy thump of his heart and with every beat she felt a wave of heat come through his tuxedo.

He sat her down on a bed in a room with clay-colored shag carpeting. The bedspread was paisley and pillow-soft.

"I miss you," David said.

"I miss you too. I can't believe you're here."

"I'm always with you."

"So am I," Will said.

Will was on her other side on the bed now. He took one of her hands, and David took the other. They both wore gold wedding bands on their ring fingers.

"Will," Lucy said. "There's something I need to tell you."

"I already know. It's okay."

"You do?"

"Kelly's fine."

"Kelly?"

"We made a beautiful daughter," Will said. He smiled and turned away. She followed his gaze to the doorway where a five-year-old blonde girl stood, on the edges of her feet. The fabric had just started to pill on the fuzzy flannel pajamas she wore. The light from the hallway was radiant and the little girl seemed to glow.

"Mommy, are you scared?" the little girl said.

Lucy's eyes flooded.

"No baby, come here," Lucy said, and it felt so natural to say it.

Her daughter ran to her. Little feet taking quick little steps. Pudgy arms reaching out. She hugged her daughter's tiny body close. When Lucy had been a little girl, she had always wanted a teddy bear that would hug her back, and this was sort of like that, but so much more. The love she felt for her daughter drowned out every other feeling. It filled the room. It filled everything that there was in Lucy's world. She promised herself she would never let go, and for what must have been an hour, she didn't. It wasn't until the glow of her love seeped away, and the warmth of her daughter's body grew chill, that Lucy opened her eyes to find herself lying on the floor of the Burnout drug den, clutching the hydrangea flower to her chest.

Just like that, it was over. The aches began to return to Lucy's body. Bile sat near her, swaying forward and back with eyelids hanging low and a gasoline-soaked sock in his hand.

There was soil on her belly. She realized that she'd pulled the flower out of its pot during her hallucination, and the pot lay in shards on the floor by her feet.

The foulness of the stinker still lingered in her mouth. Her trash bag was stowed safely behind Bile. Lucy crawled over to it and dug through until she found her toothbrush, and small sliver of soap, her only soap left for bathing. She popped the soap sliver in her mouth and chewed. Once she got a lather going she got the brush in there. She scrubbed relentlessly and when the suds would get too big she'd spit it all on the floor, and keep going. Eventually there was no suds left, just the bitter taste of soap inside her raw mouth.

Bile's eyelids eventually flickered wide.

"I watched over you," he said.

"Thank you."

"You don't have to worry."

Lucy shivered. For a brief beautiful time she had known escape, and love, and safety, but now those things were gone, and everything that she had run from was still here, still true, still too much for her heart to handle.

Bile brought the sock to his face and cupped it over his nose and mouth. He dragged in a full lungful, and she watched his ribs puff out. He stared at the ceiling as he held it in. Bile finally let his air out, and his swaying grew more pronounced. His eyelids drifted closed, then pulled themselves halfway open again, then drifted shut again.

"What does that feel like?" Lucy said, pointing to the sock in his hand.

Bile moved like he was underwater. He uncapped the jug of gasoline and dribbled a bit of gas into the sock. Bile held the sock out for Lucy.

She took it.

13

THE MORNING SUN ROASTED HILARY'S FLESH.

She lay absolutely still on her towel, with the gun at her side. Her bikini had to stay in the exact same place for her entire tanning session or her tan lines would be blurry. Blurry tan lines were for slobby girls, and Hilary was no slob. She didn't understand how other girls didn't care. Some didn't have swimsuits of their own, so they'd borrow whatever one they could get and they'd be laying out with a different-shaped suit each day. When they'd wear a low-cut top, their chests would be a mess. Who were these girls who could put up with weird triangles of paleness all over their tits? Didn't they have any self-esteem?

Hilary didn't have that problem. She knew how beautiful she was. She knew how much she deserved attention and that she was meant for greater things. People had always hated her for not having doubt in herself. They thought she was conceited but she wasn't. She was a realist. They all had eyes. They knew she was something rare, something precious, and that like it or not, they weren't. Let them hate her. It wasn't her fault who their parents were. They should just accept it. That would be the healthy thing. They were only mad because they were all unwilling to really take an honest look at themselves in the mirror, and she was always forcing them to, by simply being in the same room.

Hilary lay in the center of the empty quad. She sunbathed alone, while crowds of people stood with their towels in the hallways, waiting for the Varsity members posted at each hallway to tell them they were allowed to walk onto the quad. When one Skater girl, Marsha Buchanon, had gotten really tan, it was all the pale girls in McKinley could talk about. And there were a lot of pale girls. It had become so popular, even the darker-skinned girls started coming out too, just to socialize. They were hating it now though. They despised her for making them wait, for insisting that the sunshine was hers to enjoy alone. The halls were overstuffed with grumbling kids who kicked at the dirt, and cursed her name. She could feel the anger radiating from them, and it soothed her like a hot stone massage. It felt good to be on top again. Things were as they should be.

She tongued the borrowed tooth in her mouth. The superglue ruined her tongue for food, but it was a small price to pay for having a complete set. She had the Freak girl to thank for that. Hilary had told the girl she'd blow her brains out if she ever talked, but promised to cut her lips off first. Lucy was the only other person who knew about Hilary's missing tooth. Hilary would love to know if Lucy was still alive. She hadn't seen her since that night the goblin boy in the dress had dragged her away. Hopefully to murder her.

A drop of sweat slid down her left cheek from her upper lip. She wiped it away. Another drop dripped. She touched her hand to the wetness. When she pulled her hand away from her face, she saw red. A smear of blood across the back of her hand. Blood. She wiped it on her towel before anyone could see.

Hilary sat up in a panic and covered her nose. Was this really happening? Was she transitioning out of infection? It should have made her happy. Getting a nosebleed was what every McKinley student wanted. But Hilary had barely had a chance to capitalize on her new power. She held a hunk of machined metal in her hand that could blow holes in people with the pull of a finger. It could make people do anything she wanted. That presented a precious opportunity. She looked up to the crane arm in the sky overhead. Suddenly, there was so much to do.

Hilary looked down on everyone from her throne. It was a volleyball ref chair that she'd made the Geeks transform into a throne by covering every inch of it in broken pieces of old school trophies. It sparkled with golden light. Her towering throne had been placed in the center of the basketball court specifically for this meeting.

Below her, the leader of every gang sat around a table. She was amazed by how quickly the leaders had fallen in line. It had only been an hour and a half since her nose had bled and she'd put the word out. The only one she had the slightest respect for was Zachary the Geek. He was wearing an emerald-encrusted turban and a canary yellow robe, and he made it work. She knew she'd need him the most of any of them, and he'd probably make it through this without a bullet in the head. P-Nut, on the other hand, that mutt, she hoped he gave her a reason to shoot him. And by the look on his face, he knew it. He was regretting that he had ever asked her to be a whore. The boy was shaking in his skinny jeans. Bobby Corning was useless, but he had always adored her. Hilary knew less about the other three: Henry the Nerd, Lark the Saint, and Lips the Slut. They were replacement leaders, but they'd have to obey just the same.

Hilary tickled the hammer of the gun with her thumb. She craved to feel it blast again. She could tell that was going to be a problem for her.

Terry hopped onto the basketball court on one foot. He held a full glass of water. His injured foot was bundled in reddened gauze and athletic tape, and he kept all weight off it. He clenched his teeth and stared at the glass, careful to not let any water slosh out. She'd told him she'd shoot him in his other foot if he spilled a drop.

"It's about time, I asked for that water forever ago," Hilary said. "Why don't you pour it on your head."

Terry hesitated and she raised the gun. He promptly drenched himself. All the other gang leaders watched the leader of Varsity humiliate himself at her command, and it had to be having an effect on them.

Hilary stood up in her chair. "Whether you know it or not, all of you are guilty of disrespect." She began to gesticulate with the gun. "Payback starts now—Linda!"

Linda scurried in like a scared mouse and dropped a white envelope in front of each leader.

"In those envelopes, you'll find your instructions. From now until tomorrow afternoon, your gang is at my fucking disposal. You will do exactly as those instructions say and more, if I ask you to. Everything has to be carried out to perfection. If your gang falls short, if they screw up a single detail, I start poking holes through people. Starting with you. Any questions?"

Bobby slowly raised his hand.

"What's happening tomorrow?" he said.

Hilary smiled and cocked her gun.

"Prom."

14

WILL CLUNG TO THE COLD METAL RUNGS OF
the maintenance ladder in the elevator shaft. His old elevator
home hung by cable just below him. Lucy had to be there.

The longer he'd been in the school, the clearer it had
become that this plan had been busted from the start. The
school was too big and too dangerous for it to go right. He'd
been shocked by how many gangs were roving the halls at
night. It was as if they were bored of their usual hangouts
and they were looking for trouble, not avoiding it. By the time
Will had gotten to the plant room, his best guess to find Lucy,
it was morning, and she hadn't been there. He'd spent most
of the day hiding and contemplating the fact that Lucy could
be anywhere. She could be hiding, asleep in a locker, and he
could walk right by her and never see her again.

He had to depend on faith. It had been that thought, over
and over, that had recharged his weary body, and ejected him

back into the halls. He had to believe he would find Lucy soon. He had to believe that they were destined to be together, and that coming into McKinley, hunting for her on deadly terrain, was proof that he was worthy of that destiny.

She was in the elevator, he told himself.

He was going to do the jump, he'd done it more times than he could remember. It was nothing to him, he just had to catch his breath. The only problem was he'd been trying to do that for the last three minutes, and his breaths couldn't come fast enough. He was pushing too hard, and he knew it. He hadn't eaten or had anything to drink since he'd been outside.

Spots twinkled in his vision. He felt dizzy. The possibility crossed his mind that he could pass out and fall to his death, so he jumped. Will's heels hit the roof of the elevator car and he fell to his knees. He still couldn't catch his breath, but now he realized the air was hardly coming through the filter. Something was wrong with his mask.

The filter had to be clogged. It felt like he was underwater, breathing through a hundred-foot drinking straw. He crawled for the elevator hatch. Lucy might be inside. He was only getting air in little sips, and his exhales were bubbling. On his knees he lifted the hatch to the elevator. The exertion made his vision gray out and his head feel filled with helium. Will's muscles quit and he fell forward, straight through the hatch, and into the elevator.

His back slapped the linoleum floor, and his head followed

with a crack. By the dim emergency lights, he could see the cold truth. Lucy wasn't here. He was alone in an empty box.

He sucked in empty breaths like a dying frog. He'd been dreaming, thinking Lucy would be here. He stared at the fallen shelves he and David had put up. This was crazy. He was dying fast. He had only a trickle of air coming through, and he wasn't sure if he was imagining it. He fumbled with the front of his mask, tugging at things that wouldn't budge, trying to figure out what could be clogging his air, but it was too late. Panic was crushing his throat. His lungs were spinning, confused and hating him for not giving them air. Will ached to yank his mask off now. What was a better way to die? Silent and choking or red and explosive? He didn't have the guts to go out big. He wriggled in pain and slapped the wall with fading strength.

Time slowed, and Will realized he couldn't stop it. He became weirdly serene. His mind drifted to Lucy and the future they wouldn't have together. He saw his son. The boy looked more like Will than Lucy. Although he could see a little of her in his eyes and his hair. Will had forgotten about the natural color of Lucy's hair. It was a deep gold with traces of brown like the grain of lacquered pine. He hadn't seen her hair like that since the first day of school. The boy's golden bangs kept falling into his eyes and he couldn't be bothered with clearing them out of his way. That was just like Will. He knew in his heart, that boy would be wild.

He saw them living in a modest Pale Ridge house, a fixer-upper, with *THORPE* hand-painted on the mailbox. Lucy was good at that kind of thing. And Will had gotten good at fixing gutters and replacing windows. Even though it wasn't how he would have wanted to spend his weekends after working a boring job all week, he found joy in it, because it was his house he'd bought with his wife. He supposed that was what love was.

Every moment was precious. Will sent his son to his room for acting out, then he and Lucy chuckled about it as soon as the little rascal was gone, because the boy was just like his old man. The three of them never missed a dinner together. They'd go back for seconds and thirds of Lucy's famous cooking. They'd talk about dream vacations. They'd joke and laugh and gossip about any relative that wasn't within earshot, mainly Uncle David. Maybe Lucy would make rhubarb pie on Will's birthday. He loved rhubarb pie.

Will felt a twinge of sadness. He remembered he was dying. It wasn't fair. His life could have been so good. He would have treasured every minute. He wanted to age. He wanted to lose his hair. He wanted to lose his looks. He wanted to watch Lucy gain weight over the years. He wanted a life. But it all faded away, and for his final moments, no matter how hard he tried to wish himself back to his dream life, Will stared at the dirty, speckled elevator floor. He closed his eyes.

A heavy thump vibrated the floor.

Will's eyelids widened. His vision was murky but he saw someone in a gas mask on the floor next to him. David.

Will couldn't trust it. It had to be a dream. He watched David kneel at his side.

"Don't breathe," David said.

Don't worry, Will thought.

"Nod that you understand me."

Will managed to blink rather than nod. It seemed to be enough for David. He grabbed Will by the head and nimbly undid the filter off the front of his mask. Less than a second passed before David shoved a new one in. It locked on to the front of his mask with a plastic *click*.

Air. It flowed into Will's mask like a breeze. Will sucked in a breath so big he thought he would bust a rib. If his lungs had taste buds, he bet that first breath would have tasted like a banana split.

"You okay?" David said.

Will managed to nod. David kicked him in the liver.

"What the fuck were you thinking?" David yelled. His voice came out distorted through the small speaker by the chin of his mask.

"Hey!" Will shouted between pained breaths.

David kicked him again, this time in the shoulder.

"Cut it out!"

"Do you *ever* think? Is there anything in that fucking head of yours?"

David was leaning so far over him that he had to slide up the wall to get to his feet. David speared his finger into Will's face shield as he yelled.

"Answer me!"

Will knew he'd put his brother in a horrible position. He knew David had just saved his life. But David's finger was in his face, and Will found it so infuriating that neither of those facts seemed important.

"Go fuck yourself," Will said.

Will saw anger in David's eyes that he'd never seen before, and then David hurled his fist at Will's face. Knuckles crashed into Will's mask. Will dropped to the floor and stared in horror at the face shield to his mask.

There was a giant vertical crack in it.

"Oh shit, oh shit, oh shit," David said and dropped down beside Will.

Will couldn't move. The crack in front of his eyes was his entire world. It traveled down the plastic like a lightning bolt, angling left to right.

"I didn't mean to . . . ," David said as he dug through his backpack. "I'm sorry—don't . . . just little breaths, okay?"

Will did as David said. If that crack was enough to make David scared, then Will knew he should be shitting his pants. David pulled a disposable lighter out of his pocket.

"Stay calm. Okay? I can fix this," David said as he sparked the lighter and held the flame up to the top of the crack. Will took infant breaths as he watched the plastic begin to smoke and soften under the flame. David moved the lighter down the crack at a slug's pace, leaving a warped trail behind.

Behind David's mask, sweat fell down his face in steady streams and fogged his face shield near the temples. His anger had vaporized, replaced by emotions that Will was accustomed to seeing on his brother's face: fear and guilt.

"Come on, come on, come on," David muttered.

Why was it, Will wondered, that the moments he felt closest to his brother were the ones when they came close to killing each other?

"I think it's gonna work," David said, flicking his eye to meet Will's.

He finished melting the bottom of the crack, and Will dared to take full breaths again. His vision was now marred by a thick, blackened stripe of bubbled plastic scar tissue. If he closed his right eye, the world looked distorted. He felt like an ashtray.

David fell back against the wall with an exhausted huff, like he'd just fought off a heart attack. They looked at each other as they both gulped down air. Will couldn't help but be struck with a sense of déjà vu. Here they were again, sitting in their elevator home after a blowout fight, hiding from the rest of the school.

"Thanks," Will said.

"Sorry," David said.

"I deserved it—sort of."

David stayed quiet.

Will knew he owed David the real explanation. If there was ever a time to clear the air, it was now. Will just really wished it wasn't. He'd come into the school hoping that he wouldn't have to. He'd planned on finding Lucy and lifting them both out before David even knew he was gone, and then he'd tell him. But it didn't happen like that. He had to tell him now . . . or maybe he should warm up to it.

"How'd you find me?" Will said.

"Lucky," David said. His voice was sour.

This was going to suck.

"I didn't mean to drag you into this," Will said.

"No?"

"No, I didn't come back here just to stress you out, you know. I had a real reason—"

"You got Lucy pregnant."

He stared at David, stunned by the very truth he was about to reveal. David shook his head.

"Goddamn it, Will."

Will instinctively reached for his forehead to ease the tension in his head, but his hand bounced off his gas mask.

"I'm sorry," Will said. "It was an accident."

"No shit?"

Will sighed. David was going to be mad at him forever.

"How did you—how did you find out?" Will said.

"Saw Mort. I guess everybody knows you and Lucy were together," David said. Disappointment dripped from his every word. "I guessed the rest."

They sat in silence again.

"You should have told me," David said.

Will met David's indignant eye. He saw what he'd been dreading there, what he'd been hoping to avoid—betrayal. Stabbed in the back by his own flesh and blood.

"We thought you were dead," Will said in a rush.

"Yeah, I got that part."

"It's not like either of us thought we were going behind your back."

"So, then, I've got no right to be upset? Is that what you're saying?"

"I guess I'm saying . . . ," Will paused and wondered why he was holding back. "I'm saying, join the club. I was in love with Lucy first, and that didn't stop you from moving in on her."

"I said I was sorry about that, back then," David said.

"Yeah, and I said sorry just now. Does that make you any less pissed off?"

David's face was puckered with a frown. Will knew he was bringing up ancient history, but he needed David to understand that when it came to Lucy, Will won. David could be as hurt as he wanted to be. What Will and Lucy had was deeper. That was just the way it was.

"Ever heard of condoms?" David said.

Will wanted to fire something back, but his child's life hung in the balance. Everything wasn't about Will anymore.

"I'm sorry," Will said.

"What?" David's tone was aggravated but his face was scrunched up in confusion. Clearly, Will apologizing was a new experience for him.

"I know we had it good out there on the farm. It was great. I didn't mean to fuck it up. I didn't mean for any of this to happen. I'm just trying to do the right thing."

David stared at him with the same confusion, but only for a few more seconds before he closed his eyes and sighed. He exhaled, and all the tension in his body seemed to exit with his breath.

"I know," David said. He massaged his neck. "I know you are."

David had forgiven him after arguments in this elevator so many times in the past. Their love for each other would always be stronger than any conflict that came between them.

"Hey, remember when I wanted to knock a hole in the floor so we wouldn't have to leave to go to the bathroom?" Will said.

One side of David's mouth tilted up.

"How long did we fight about that?" Will said.

"Four months? Five?"

Will chuckled. "I still say it's way more convenient. You'd only have to go into the school for food!"

"I can't believe you want to get into this—what don't you

understand about me not wanting to watch you shit? About my house smelling like your ass?" David said, his smile widening.

"So the other person has to go up top and not come back till the smell's gone. Is that so bad?"

"What about the giant pile of it that would build up at the bottom of the shaft? That would stink the whole shaft up."

"I never smelled anything."

"What does that mean?"

"I don't think that's a real problem, that's all I'm sayin'."

"Did you crap off the roof?" David said, pointing above.

"Well . . . yeah, I always figured you did too, but that we both kinda knew not to talk about it," Will said.

"No, I did not do that! I went to the bathroom like a human being." David laughed. "What's wrong with you? It's like living with a gorilla. How many of your turds are down there right now?" David said.

"Ballpark? Hmm. Let me think. I'm not great with math."

"You have to use math?"

"I think I could guess my average weekly total. And if I multiply it out . . ."

"Jesus Christ, that means like every day. If you have weekly totals, that means pretty much daily."

Will couldn't stop laughing from how riled up David was getting. David was laughing in bursts, between stretches of mock outrage.

"No, okay, I'll be honest," Will said. "If I really had to put a number on it, conservatively I'd say thirty-five."

"Thirty-five! Are you being for real?"

Will was being for real. Thirty-five was his best estimate.

"Yeah. About."

David laughed and shook his head. He threw his hands up in the air. "I give up," he said. "You are a maniac."

"I like to be comfortable, that's all. Hard to relax in the bathrooms when you always have to watch your back."

David smiled, but he didn't say anything back. Will didn't know what to say next either. The jovial mood began to fade, but it wasn't uncomfortable. It was normal. Will really was sorry he'd dragged his brother into this, but he couldn't deny that he was relieved to have him here.

"I hate the idea of Lucy alone in here," David said.

"It kills me."

"Let's go find her," David said.

"You mean that? With two of us, we can definitely do it."

"Definitely," David said, but he didn't get up.

Will didn't move either. With David behind him, he felt a renewed confidence, but his body felt like a bag of sludge. He'd been going full throttle for a day straight, and it was taking its toll.

"I just need to catch my breath," Will said.

"Tell me about it."

Will closed his eyes for a second.

15

DAVID OPENED HIS EYE TO THE BRUSHED
steel wall of the elevator. He'd had nightmares on the outside that had started like this. Back in school again. But this
was no dream. He reached up to wipe the sleep from his eyes
and the drool from his chin, but his fingers hit his face
shield. He was still half asleep. His filtered breath echoed in
his ears.

He looked at his watch: 9:05 a.m. David scrambled up to a
seated position, his back against the wall.

No. That couldn't be right. He looked at his watch again.
He tapped on it with one finger. The digital seconds clicked
along without a care for him or his rising panic. David looked
over at Will. He was in a heavy sleep.

"Oh shit," David said and stood. "SHIT!"

Will jumped awake.

"What the fuck?" Will said.

"Get up," David said.

"I am up."

"No, I mean, stand up. Let's go. We gotta go."

Will blinked a few times and shook his head like a dog. He stared at the floor, confused and groggy.

"Now!" David said and reached down to take his hand. He pulled Will up.

"What's going on?"

"It's morning. We slept through the night."

"What?! You didn't set an alarm or something?"

"I slept through it. I guess we were more wiped out than we thought. We've been running around with no water and . . ."

"Fuck!" Will said.

David pulled on his backpack. He dragged the milk-crate stepping stool to the middle of the elevator and got up on it. He slid the hatch open, and they made their way out of the elevator. Every movement was sloppy. His mind was moving twice as fast as his body.

"We'll find her," Will said when they made it to the hallway.

But they didn't. As they searched, David watched the hours slip away until noon. Room after room and hallway after hallway, they didn't find a trace of her, or get anything close to a lead. Eventually the halls started to blend together until it became hard to remember which ones they'd already explored. The time they had to spend hiding from people aggravated David, because they weren't making progress, but he wasn't sure that they were making progress the rest of the time either.

The two of them crept down another hall, side by side.

"Did you ever miss it?" Will said after a while.

"Miss what?"

"McKinley."

David gave Will a look.

"Yeah, I'd write about it in my journal every night."

"Really?"

"No. Why would I miss being locked up with no daylight and no food?"

Will shrugged. "There's more going on in here than that. You were a rock star for a while. You aren't that outside. You're hanging out with a bunch of fifty-year-olds, shucking corn."

David passed a decrepit classroom. He remembered what Mort had told him in the Stairs, that sometimes, he would go to the old Loners' turf when he needed to relive happier times. He'd been moved when he'd heard that, but he didn't feel that way now. He felt sad.

"I think we were all making the best of a bad—"

Will grabbed David's arm and pulled him back from the corner they were about to turn.

"Ssh," he said. "Look at that."

Will pointed at the darkened doorways of the two class-rooms nearest to them in the long hallway ahead. The classrooms were populated by ghostly figures. Freaks. They all held weapons. They were hiding. Waiting.

Two Nerds walked into the hall at the other end. They each shouldered plump bags from the food drop, and were chatting. He shared a worried look with Will. He was about to witness another mugging. Would he stand by and just let it happen again? But when the Nerds passed the occupied classrooms, the Freaks did nothing. The Nerds walked on, unaware of the danger they'd avoided.

"What's going on?" Will whispered.

"I don't get it," David said.

But then, he did.

A giant group of Skaters rolled into the hall from the same direction the Nerds had. It was nearly the whole gang, fresh from the quad, lugging their gang's entire food drop ration. This was what the Freaks had been waiting for, a big score.

The Freaks pounced. There were so many. They leapt from their hiding spots, and burst out of classrooms to pummel the unsuspecting Skaters with baseball bats and two-by-fours. Food scattered onto the floor. A Freak threw a brick down onto the face of a tripped Skater and snatched the bunch of carrots from his hands. He saw a Skater girl get a knife in the shoulder. The Skaters tried to fight back, but they'd been caught off guard, and they couldn't reverse the momentum. The food on the floor was snatched up by the Freaks, and once they had most of it, they fled, leaving the Skaters to pick up the remnants of their rations and hobble off home.

David's spirits sank. He'd been so proud of what he and the parents had done on the farm. He'd believed the food drops had been made peaceful, and that he was helping turn McKinley into a safer place, but now he understood. The violence hadn't been neutralized, it had only been pushed inside.

The brothers soldiered on, continuing their search, and Will started talking to him about some bullshit, but David wasn't paying attention. He couldn't stop thinking about how ignorant he and the parents were of what it was actually like in McKinley, and how their sense of control over the quarantine was only an illusion.

"...I mean, where did Hilary even get a loaded gun?"

"What?" David said. He turned to face Will. "What are you talking about?"

"Yeah. I heard a bunch of people talking about it. She's got a loaded gun and she declared herself queen."

David felt like he'd just been shoved off a cliff. Hilary with a gun. Hilary with power over everyone. How long would it take for her to find out he was here? How long would it take for her to send everyone after him, just like Sam had done? Goddamn it—he hated this school. What the fuck was he still doing here, he had to find Lucy and get out now.

David got kicked out of his thoughts when he heard a disembodied voice call out, seemingly from nowhere.

"Gas masks!" the voice said.

David tensed. There was no one else in the hallway but him and Will.

"Who said that?" Will said.

All the lockers around them sprung open. Forty Geeks, twenty on each side, bounded out of the lockers. They surrounded David and Will.

"Give us those gas masks," a Geek with a knife said.

"Wait," David said. "You don't understand."

"I understand they're rare as shit and we're gonna get so much food for—" The Geek's eyes went wide. "Hoh . . . ," he said. "You're David."

"It is!" another said. "No way! And Will too."

"If we get separated, meet at the elevator," David whispered to Will.

The Geeks touched David. They touched his mask. Alien tribesmen meeting their first astronaut. David jerked away from one, only to end up in the hands of another.

"Hands off!" Will said.

"Tell us everything," one said to David. "What's going on out there?"

"It's . . . ," David said. They tugged on his arms. On his bag. He could feel someone unzipping his backpack. Where the crane remote was. He shook them off his bag, but Geeks were crowding between him and Will, and David didn't like it.

"We're leaving now," David said.

"Leaving the school?" one said with excitement.

"Can you get us out?" another said.

"Is it over? Is the quarantine over?"

"It's all over," one shouted. "It's gotta be!"

"David's come back and he's going to let us out!" a Geek yelled like he was trying to tell the whole school. Other Geeks came out of hiding spots all down the hall and hustled over. The crowd around them grew.

"That's not what's happening," David tried to say, but the idea had caught on too fast. The Geeks were already yelling over him.

"We're getting out! We're finally getting out!"

People from other gangs came running from halls and classrooms, breathless at the news. Four Saints came rushing around the corner. A group of Sluts appeared. Six Varsity came jogging up. He saw others approaching from the distance.

David's eyes jerked to Will, and he saw the panic rising in his brother.

Will face-palmed a Geek into the lockers. "Run!" he yelled, and bolted away.

David wanted to run after Will, but there were too many people between them.

"Don't let him go!" Geeks said, and grabbed for him.

David jumped out of reach, and was able to sprint away—in the opposite direction of Will.

16

LUCY WOULD NEVER THINK OF GASOLINE THE
same way. If she ever made it out of McKinley and had a real
life again, she'd probably hit the gas station every day and
top off her tank, just to be around the wonderful smell. She
pressed her gas-soaked rag over her mouth and nose and
sucked, already anticipating the numbing haze that would
descend on her.

She watched one of the Burnout girls squat down and piss
on the floor of the hallway, with her shorts bunched at her
knees. The urine pooled by the girl's bare feet, which were black
with grime. The girl's eyelids were drooping, she looked on the
verge of falling asleep. She showed no embarrassment that
other people could see her. She even seemed bored. She pulled
her shorts back on with no underwear and without dabbing herself dry. It meant nothing to this girl. It meant nothing to Lucy
either, now that the gasoline fumes were swirling in her chest.

Lucy let out a breath and felt the ground begin to pull away from her feet. Dizzy, she had to grab Bile's bony shoulder to keep from falling. The high she got from the gasoline fogged the world around her. As soon as the fog showed hints of clearing, she'd ask Bile to dribble more gas on her rag, and he'd look at her like a proud parent, then gladly oblige. That's how it had gone for hours. She wasn't sure how many. She just wanted to keep this feeling, or lack of feeling, going for as long as she could.

Bile touched her lightly on the small of her back, letting her know he was there to catch her again if she needed him to. He'd proven to her that he would keep her safe. Any one of the other Burnouts who tried to mess with her in the hours she'd been on this bender received a minor beating from Bile, or the threat of one. She knew what it looked like when a guy wanted to protect her.

They were in Skater territory, near P-Nut's strip club. From what Lucy had heard weeks ago, the strip club was a joke, just one room where three or four girls danced in underwear with pillowcases over their heads to protect their reputations. For all the hype and promotion P-Nut had been doing over the PA system, the strip club hadn't amounted to much. Kids weren't rich like they'd been in the Gates days. Fewer and fewer people had extra food to throw away on a little look-but-don't-touch action.

One of the other Burnouts—she'd heard Bile call him

Clive—was selling homemade drugs. He wore a jean jacket with a dozen panties stapled to the front. His belt was two toy rubber snakes tied together. He wore black sunglasses in the dark hall. A Skater walked up to Clive.

"What are you selling?" the Skater said.

"Burners. Clouds," Clive said.

"Are those new?"

"Blows my old shit out of the water."

Clive pulled something out of his pocket. In his palm were a crusty cotton ball and a cigarette made out of notebook paper.

"Burners are the cigarettes, and they speed things up, makes things intense, y'know. These balls are called clouds. You light this up, inside a bag, or a bucket or something, and stick your head in that smoke, you won't be feelin' dick."

"Cool, cool," the Skater said, "I'll take two clouds."

"Smart man."

Lucy wanted two clouds too, but she didn't want to owe Clive anything. He looked at her like she was a house of cards that he wanted to blow over. A nervous Freak walked up to Clive, looking over his shoulder the whole time like he was afraid of being seen.

"Hey, somebody told me I should come here for some, ya know, satisfaction."

"Yeah, sure," Clive said to the Freak. "Just wait over there."

Clive pointed to the classroom where Lucy and Bile were standing. The Freak walked over to them, and stared at

Lucy's breasts like he could see through her shirt. He smiled at her.

"All right, nice," the Freak said. "We're gonna have fun."

He reached out to touch her. Lucy didn't move. She wondered what would happen. Would she care if he squeezed her? Would she like it?

Bile stepped between Lucy and the Freak.

"Three cans," he said, his voice slow and lilting.

"Yeah, fine," the Freak said and produced the payment.

"In there," Bile said and thumbed the Freak toward the classroom.

The Freak smiled at Lucy.

"See you inside," he said and walked in.

Bile planted two fingers in his mouth and let out a sharp whistle.

A girl walked out from behind the row of lockers across the hall. The others called her Horse, and she looked like a body that had washed up on a riverbank. Her hair was a bird's nest, her eyes were sunken pits, and her skin looked like it was having an allergic reaction to her life. She wore a flower-print dress. Horse didn't look at Lucy or Bile as she followed the Freak into the room and shut the door.

Part of Lucy was appalled. Somewhere in the depths of her mind Lucy knew that what was about to happen in that room, what she'd seen Horse do three times already, was wrong. But that part of her that objected was small and feeble-voiced and just barely rising into her consciousness. Bile doused the gas rag again and put it to her face. She clutched his hands in hers, tighter this time, and inhaled. That small part of her drifted away again.

Bile turned to Lucy and smiled. His inflamed gums seemed to be fleeing his teeth.

"You'd fit in great with us," he said.

"I would?"

"Most folks think we're crap, but you don't judge us like that."

She could hear the boy in the classroom start to grunt with passion. Horse never made a noise.

"I don't judge people."

That wasn't true. Lucy judged people all the time. A week ago, she wouldn't have hesitated to call Bile and these Burnouts degenerates. She tried not to think about it. She saw a glimmer of gold from the necklace around his neck.

"What was she like? Your mom," Lucy said.

Bile was momentarily shocked. Conflicting emotions flickered across his face.

"Was she nice?" Lucy asked.

"You really want to know?"

"Sure."

He smiled. "She was . . . gentle as a feather. She never thought bad of me, no matter what I did. Like you."

"Like me?"

"Yeah," Bile said, then he started to whisper. "You're . . . you're the only one who knows."

"Knows what?"

He wouldn't meet her eyes. He scratched at the open sores on his shoulder.

"Where I came from, and how I got here and all."

It was strange. Lucy had found it so easy to forget that Bile had been the one that infected the whole school. Lucy stared at his hideous face. Every kid Bile saw, every hall he walked through, had to remind him of what he'd done. He'd destroyed the world.

"Did you mean to?" Lucy said. "Do this?"

Bile didn't answer. He looked around at the holes knocked in the walls, the checkerboard of missing ceiling panels above them. From inside the classroom behind them they could hear the boy's dirty talk. "Yeah, bitch. Take that shit. Take that shit, you dirty bitch. Fuck yeah. You love that shit, don't you?"

"I was scared," Bile said.

She heard the Freak finish in the other room.

"It's okay," Lucy said. She reached out and touched the paper skin of Bile's arm.

A low moan crept out of his throat.

"Ssh, it's okay," she said, even though she wasn't sure if it was okay at all, or whether he should ever be forgiven for what he'd put them through, but it was the nice friend thing to say, and right now, Bile was her only friend.

He threw his spindly arms around her and squeezed. His breathing came staggered with sobs. His body twitched and shook so hard it reminded her of one of Will's seizures. Lucy slowly lifted her arms and wrapped them around him in a half-committed hug. The Freak brushed past them as he left the classroom behind. The clank of his belt buckle as he fastened his pants sickened Lucy like a penny in her mouth.

They all headed back to the ruins. Bile kept touching her as they walked. Brushing up against her. Putting an arm across her chest to stop her from walking around a corner until he'd checked whether it was safe. And the way he looked at her had changed. He was eager to smile at her, and she would smile back, but she couldn't hold his gaze as long as he wanted to. It seemed that he wanted them to gaze into each other's eyes without end. Lucy could fake that for a little while longer, but what would be next? She didn't want to feel the hard, cracked skin of his lips if he planted a surprise kiss on her, or the scrape of his torn fingernails on her breast if he groped her.

She was thinking more clearly now. That wasn't good. She wanted the numbness back. By the time they made it back to the single ruined room where Bile and the other Burnouts ate, drank, slept, and huffed, Lucy was dangerously close to stone-cold sober.

She sat on a backpack full of empty water bottles, with her back to the sticky wall. The room stank of armpits and sour breath and clogged toilets. She looked around and saw vacant eyes peering at nothing, faces sagging toward the floor. Bottles of sewage stacked by the wall. Horse sat crumpled up in the corner, plucking her eyelashes out one by one.

Lucy shifted her weight. She felt cold. The aches of her battered body made themselves known to her again. She groaned softly. Her brain volunteered memories she yearned to forget. She shook her head.

Bile sauntered into the room with a newfound confidence. He held a stinker in each hand. The soup of human waste sloshed around inside the bottles, and the inflated latex gloves wobbled from side to side like they were waving at her.

"Where's the gas?" she said. Her voice was desperate.

"Running low," he said. "We have to save it."

He plopped down beside her with an assured grin that was almost suave. He extended one of the stinkers out to her. Lucy clamped her mouth and turned away. The urge to vomit was barely containable. She closed her eyes. She saw her child twitch in her hands. She put her head between her knees.

"Need a minute," she said and blew out a long breath.

"You don't mind, do you?" he said, holding up the other bottle.

Lucy shook her head. She could feel Bile's elbow rub up and down her thigh as he twisted the base of the glove. She could hear the light snap of rubber as he pulled the glove off the bottle, the squeak as he tied it off like a birthday balloon.

Lucy dared to look up at him. She pinched her nose shut. Bile grabbed the middle finger of the engorged glove and bit the tip off. He sucked in the methane, squeezing the life out of the glove to make sure he didn't waste any.

She thought he'd never exhale. She watched his eyeballs roll back until she could see only the bloodshot whites of his eyes behind fluttering eyelids. Finally his jaw drifted down and his lips pulled apart. Foul air spilled from his mouth. He moaned from deep in his chest and it sounded like a colony of bats escaping a cave.

When his corneas sank back into view, he stared through her, at something far away. Thick spit dripped off his lip like glue.

"You're here," he slurred.

She had to cover her nose from the rank smell of his toilet breath.

"Where else would I be?" Lucy said.

"I missed you so much," Bile said.

"Are you all right?"

Of course he wasn't all right. She remembered her own experience with stinkers, and she knew whoever Bile thought he was talking to, it wasn't her.

He grabbed her hand.

"Momma," he said.

The word formed icicles in her stomach. She tried to yank her hand away, but his grip was iron.

"Bile, let me go."

She felt her stomach acid climb her throat. She yanked and yanked but his fingers dug into her wrist like tent stakes.

"I love you, Mommy," he said.

She punched him in the ear. It hurt her knuckles, but he let go. His eyes were wide like a little boy's. Tears spilled.

"Why'd you hit me? Why are you mad at me?"

Lucy ran out of the room. She dashed down ruined hallways, knocking into rubble, fleeing the sound of his voice.

"Please don't go, Momma, I'm sorry!" he shrieked after her. "I didn't mean to do it, Momma. I didn't!"

17

THE HALLWAY WAS AS EMPTY AS HER UTERUS.

Lucy wept, curled in a ball, inside a hall so dark she couldn't see a foot in front of her face. Only the ceiling lights at each end of the forty feet of hallway were operational. Her wet hair clung to her cheeks. She couldn't understand how she had gotten to this point. What had happened to her life? She used to have friends, a gang, a place to sleep, the food she needed. Now life was an unending horror show, and she didn't know how much more she could take.

Mommy.

Bile's broken voice echoed through her skull.

The thought of her baby-that-would-never-be drove more tears from her eyes. She couldn't help but blame herself. Maybe all the bad things that had happened were her fault. Maybe they'd grown out of her cowardice. She'd hid behind David in the Loners. Behind Violent in the Sluts. And now she was clinging to Bile the same way. Maybe if she'd stood on her own two feet for once, this wouldn't be where she was right now. Maybe the universe was punishing her, taking everything possible from her until she toughened up. No. That didn't make any sense. Lucy wasn't thinking straight.

She wished Violent were there to tell her what to do. She wished Violent were alive. She wished it wasn't her fault that Violent was dead.

Lucy kicked a nearby closet door. She heard it clap against the closet wall, then drift back on vibrating hinges. She couldn't get ahold of herself. Her anguish wouldn't release its grip on her. She wanted it all to stop. She wished there was a way she could escape the pain and leave it all behind.

Her bladder cried out to her. She had to pee. Lucy stood up and walked through the dark, toward a bathroom ahead, arms outstretched and waving through the air like insect antennae. Lucy heard the creak of the bathroom door. Blaring light streamed out of the bathroom in front of her as the door swung open. Figures filed out, backlit by the bathroom, their translucent white hair glowing atop their heads.

Saints.

Lucy froze. And so did they. She was lit up like a fugitive in a spotlight. They pushed her up against the wall. There had to be fifteen of them. Different pairs of hands pressed her into the wall. They were all in her face, staring at her like she was a silverfish in their soup. One of them held open the bathroom door to keep light on the situation. Their faces crowded around her, eyes hid under long shadows.

They berated her, said vicious things. They mocked her and ripped her clothes. A tiny, bird-boned hand reached out and clamped Lucy's neck. It belonged to Lark. She leaned in close, into the light from the bathroom. Dark circles stained the skin under Lark's eyes. Her hair was a mess, roughly collected in a rubber band atop her head. The fingernails on the hand that wasn't choking Lucy had been gnawed down to gummy crescents of red enflamed skin. Her middle fingertip was bleeding, and there was a string of thinned blood framing her upper lip. Her eyes seemed to swirl.

"I've been waiting for this," Lark said.

"Wait. No, you have it wrong."

"Did you kill Gates?" Lark frothed.

"Yes, but—" Lucy said.

"Then how do I have it wrong?"

Lark flashed her eyes as if to dare Lucy to speak.

"Because . . . ," Lucy said, swallowing hard to wet her dry throat. "Gates wasn't who you thought he was. He snapped. He killed your friend Pruitt."

The other Saints eyed each other with doubt. By the way they were reacting they might already have suspected that fact, or known it. Lark slapped Lucy in the face with the heel of her palm. Lucy's ear buzzed. Her cheek flared hot.

"Gates was a hero," Lark whispered.

The Saints nodded, until Lark pulled out a buck knife. The blade had seen heavy use, its finish was dull, and the cutting edge was bent and wiggly. Lark pressed the misshapen blade into the softness of Lucy's neck.

"Gates was my friend," Lark said. Her voice chugged like a steam engine. Tears streamed down her cheek. "I loved him."

"I'm sorry," Lucy said. She meant it. She could feel the first drip of blood roll hot down her neck. "I'm so sorry."

"Sorry won't bring him back."

"Take it easy, Lark," one of the Saints said. They were looking to each other now, wondering who would stop her. This was apparently more than they'd bargained for.

"He'd want me to do this," Lark said. "You know he'd want revenge. We owe it to him."

Lark locked eyes with Lucy again and tensed her wrist. Now was the time to fight back, this was the moment, and yet she didn't. Something inside her gave way. A long straining muscle finally went slack. She allowed an idea to enter her mind, and it shocked her how amenable she was to it. The pain could all stop right here. The knife could end it.

The thunder of approaching footsteps filled the silence. All heads turned to peer at the hall's end where the ceiling light worked and the area was bathed in a bright light.

A boy in a gas mask ran around the corner.

A clamoring crowd was right on his heels. Lucy focused on the prey, but the masked boy ran past the lit section and into the dark belly of the hallway, becoming one with the darkness. She watched the crowd follow. A constant river of faces, each defined in brilliant light for a brief moment before slipping into the black. They were mostly Geeks. Lucy felt the Saints' grip on her relax. They were clearly as dumbfounded as she was. Saints whipped out their phones. Nine smartphones shone their wan light toward the oncoming stampede, illuminating nothing, but casting a pale glow that only made it harder to see, like a film of milk glazed over the scene.

The masked boy burst into the light from the open bathroom, colliding with a few Saints, and then dashed past. In the second that he was fully illuminated, Lucy could see right into his mask.

Lucy saw an eye patch.

18

THE SAINTS TOPPLED LIKE CANDLESTICK PINS
as the rushing crowd barreled down the hallway. One Saint
held onto Lucy longer than the others, but the current of
bodies knocked him down, too. He almost pulled Lucy to the
ground with him. When the cotton of her shirt slipped out of
his grip, she burst forward like a sprinter out of the starter
blocks. Lucy lost herself in the confusion of the speeding
mob.

It couldn't be.

But she'd seen it. She knew she had. In that blur of a moment,
she'd seen a black eye patch. She wasn't sure about the
guy's face. When she tried to summon a mental image of
the face she'd glimpsed, it was a hazy and shifting blob. But
who else could it be? Who else would come back into this
school? It was the scenario Lucy'd dreamed about, but it had
been so long since she'd had those dreams because it was

impossible. David was dead. He'd been dead for months. He hadn't dug himself out of the grave. Zombies weren't real. David wasn't Jesus. It had to have been someone else with an eye patch.

Grunts. Heavy breathing. Screeching sneakers. Lucy fought her way toward the front of the pack. The mob hooked around a corner, past a melted plastic display case full of black-and-white photos of old school plays. She realized her aches and pains had evaporated.

She saw David. Or whoever it was. For a flash, she saw his back before he rushed around another dark corner thirty feet ahead. She lusted to grab this guy by the shoulders, whip him around, and stare through that mask. Her mind had become very clear. For the first time in weeks, life didn't seem so futile. Gone was her inner conviction that every road would end down for her. If David was alive and he was here, then everything would be all right. She knew it would, if he was here. The last time she had felt truly safe had been with David, and she had never allowed herself to admit that fact until now, because it was too sad, because it could never happen again, because he was dead. Now, he might be alive, with a fifty-foot lead, doing his best to get the hell away from her.

The kid who might be David slammed into a door frame ahead and then scurried into a classroom. Lucy and the mob rammed toward the classroom and clogged the doorway.

Stuck inside the knot of bodies in the doorway, Lucy spotted a pair of legs hanging out of a fractured hole in the classroom's ceiling. The legs swayed and kicked as their owner climbed up a wobbling orange extension cord that hung down through the hole.

Lucy slipped out of the knot of bodies, just as it was starting to pop through the doorway. She was the first to grab the extension cord. It swung with her weight, and the Geeks trailing her tumbled down as they grabbed for the cord and missed.

The masked boy's feet were already too high to grab, but she would've if she could've. She hoisted herself up with a tremendous pull. She felt the cord jerk with new weight below her. The Geeks were getting a grip now.

The extension cord was knotted every two feet with handholds like a rope swing. Above, she saw that there was another hole hacked through the second-floor ceiling, and the knotted extension cord hung from the third-floor ceiling like a gymnasium climbing rope. The masked boy didn't look down. Lucy climbed, gripping knots in her hands and clamping them between the insteps of her feet. The climb was hard. It didn't help that kids were fighting each other to be next up the rope, and she swore she could feel someone tugging on her clothes.

Lucy breached the hole in the ceiling. Her head was now on the second floor. The walls of this second-floor classroom were papered with photographs of grass and foliage from textbooks. There was a picnic blanket laid out in the middle of the room with a cracked acoustic guitar on top of it. The boy in the mask was waist-high into the third floor and climbing. She saw the bottom of his boots above her head and wondered whether those were the kind of shoes David would choose if he were on the outside.

Her arms caught fire as she urged them to not give up. Her forearms protested but she didn't listen. She could feel muscle fibers giving up all across her back, she felt a shard of glass forming in the meat of her left bicep, but she wasn't going to give in to cramps and fatigue.

Overhead, the masked boy swung a foot onto the third floor, got his weight over his feet, and dashed away.

"Wait," Lucy cried, but he was gone.

The weight of the Geeks below her pulled the cord straighter than a fireman's pole. Lucy kept climbing, acid in her arms, until she pulled herself up to the third floor. She reached out for the edge of the ragged hole and grasped a piece of rebar that jutted out from the crumbling concrete. She transferred her other hand from the cord to the bar, with half her weight still resting on the knot in between her shoes. The knot's resistance dropped away from her feet.

Too many kids climbing at once. The cord had been tied to a sprinkler pipe on the ceiling of the third floor. The slender metal bracket that had fastened the pipe to the ceiling couldn't withstand the weight. The pipe had ripped out of the ceiling and bent toward the floor, dumping the cord right off the end of the pipe. It slipped away and fell.

She heard the other climbers crunch into the floor and wail in agony. Her weight pulled on her fingers, and tried to pop her knuckles apart. The rebar was cold, and rough, and angled down into the hole. Water burst from the broken sprinkler pipe above, spitting onto her. The water slicked the rebar, and Lucy felt her grip sliding down its length.

A minute before, she had felt ready to face death. The prospect of it had seemed like a relief, but now everything was different. She was dumbfounded that she had ever felt that way. She wanted to live. She wanted to cling to life with everything in her, to hang on until the end, and to wring every drop of happiness out of it before her time was up.

Her hands slid. The moans of the injured kids two floors down beckoned her to fall. She wanted to take one of her hands off the bar and reach for the edge of the floor but she knew that she couldn't support her full weight with one hand. The bar would tear itself out of her fingers. She'd drop, accelerate to her death, and make a pretty mess on the floor. Her whimpers echoed. She slipped.

A hand grabbed her wrist.

She looked up.

It was David.

He grasped her forearm with both hands and pulled her

up. They flopped back onto the floor once her knees cleared the hole. She rested on top of him, her arms planted over his shoulders. There was his face, better than she remembered. His features richer than they'd ever been.

A dam shattered in her heart. The love she had hidden away and had tried to forget came flooding through her. Looking into his eyes she felt the familiar jolt of connection. Her attraction to him was automatic. She had no control over it, and she'd forgotten how it felt to want someone so viscerally that thought never entered the picture.

"Where have you been?" she said.

David cracked a little smile and stared at her. He wrapped his arms around her and laid both hands on the small of her back.

"Back at you," he said.

The desire was there. A tickle up her spine that told her he wanted her as much as she wanted him. It was the only way to explain how they could look at each other like this, like they were lying in a wildflower meadow with no one around for miles. The moaning two floors down and the hiss of spraying water were nothing more than ambient noise. All Lucy knew was the strength of David's arms and the warmth of his smile. She leaned closer to kiss him, but the tip of her nose pushed into the clear plastic of his face mask.

David pushed Lucy off him. She rolled onto her back. Jarred by his sudden change, she lifted herself up onto her elbows and looked at him. "We've gotta move," David said. "They'll be coming up the stairs."

He got to his feet and pulled her up. He put his hand between her shoulder blades for a gentle push forward, and she melted. David's touch made her feel high again. She was transported back to a time when she had needed no shell to protect her, before she'd been hardened by the Sluts, back to when she'd been just a girl.

David led Lucy out of the third floor classroom and into the hall. To their right were the building's foyer and the main staircase down into the school. He pulled her toward the stairs, but the thunder of footsteps echoing up made him freeze.

"Shit," David said. He looked down the hall to their left and gritted his teeth. "We're screwed."

"What's wrong?" he said, looking back at her.

Lucy was staring at a sign scratched into an upturned table. It warned about the hallway that stretched out to their left. The only place to go. *Past this point-DEATH* it said.

"Come on," Lucy said, and started in that direction.

"We can't," David said, resisting. "It's booby-trapped."

"Yeah, and I know where. Come on, they won't come looking in this direction."

David looked at her like he wasn't so sure he should be letting Lucy take the lead. He was the rescuer, after all. Not her.

"Trust me," she said.

Lucy tugged David toward the rigged hallway that led to the library. She wasn't as entirely positive as she'd let on about what traps were where, but she thought that up to the end of the first row of lockers was safe.

"Here," she said, and they tucked into the darkness where the locker row ended.

Kids stampeded up from the main staircase and into the hall. Lucy closed her eyes and held her breath until the clomping of feet faded. She opened one eye and looked at David.

"They're gone," he said, "but we should stay put, just in case they come back."

David kept his body only an inch from hers and never let her hands go. She was happy for that. His fingers stayed intertwined with hers. David's breath whistled softly through his gas mask. She stared at him, and every minute or so, his good eye would flick from its diligent watch on the hall, back to her.

"Why did you come back?" Lucy whispered. She only wanted to hear one thing.

"To find you."

Lucy sighed and smiled. "I never believed you were dead. Not really."

David's face became stern. His eye flicked back down the hall.

"I can't take credit for coming in here," he said, his voice dropping to a grave octave. "That was all Will."

Lucy felt like she was going to faint. She rested all her weight against the locker.

"Will came too?" she said with barely any breath.

Lucy knew in an instant why David's face had gone stern. She'd said she had never believed David was dead, but if that was true, she would have never fallen for Will. Suddenly, she was aware of all the awful things David must have thought about her for hooking up with his brother.

"What did Will say—"

"Shh," David said, and Lucy realized she'd blurted it at full volume.

Lucy heard feet shuffling near the entrance of the hall, but they faded off down the main stairs.

David looked back at Lucy. She loved him. She should have felt wretched about it because she cared so much about Will. Why hadn't Will even crossed her mind since she'd laid eyes on David? It was because, with Will, things had to be very particular. Stars had to align for her to love him, and even still, she'd always felt a flicker of doubt. With David, there were no special circumstances. If anything, the world fell away. There was no debate, her body made the choice, and her mind shut up.

She couldn't feel sorry about that. It was what he did to her.

"Where's Will now?" Lucy asked.

"I don't know. We got split up. Are you okay?"

"Yeah, sure."

"Is the baby okay?"

Lucy stared at David. Her brain went haywire, trying to make sense of—and then she knew.

"Belinda," she muttered.

Her old friend had come through, and Lucy had stopped believing in a rescue party the minute Belinda was out of sight. But now they were here, looking for a pregnant girl to save, and she was about to be a disappointment.

"I—"

She couldn't look David in the eye anymore. She was so ashamed. When she'd given up hope, David had been here risking his life for her. And Will . . .

"What did you mean, this was all Will?" she asked.

"Will dropped in here after . . . I told him it was too dangerous."

"You tried to stop him?"

"Wasn't exactly my finest moment," he said. "But I didn't know the baby was his. He wasn't going to let anything get in the way of keeping you safe."

Poor Will.

David put his hand on her shoulder as he continued, "He was right. I was wrong."

"I lost it," she said. She had to say it. She couldn't lie to him.

"Hmm?"

Lucy didn't want to say the word, and when she forced herself, she started to cry.

"The baby, David. I lost the baby."

Her insides twisted up. She dealt the locker an angry blow. She saw David take a little step back, away from her. Would he not love her anymore now that he'd seen what she'd become?

She didn't want him to see her ugliness, but she couldn't help it. Losing her baby was a wound that would not close. It wouldn't even scab over. It stayed wet and skinless and raw to the slightest touch. Lucy yearned for the day that it would merely be a scar.

"I'm sorry," David said.

"Nothing to do about it now," she said softly.

"You can't tell Will."

Lucy looked up.

"But—" she said.

"It'll destroy him," he said.

19

THE DANGER MADE WILL FASTER. HE WAS
sucking in hard breaths, working twice as hard as his pursu-
ers to drag air through the mask's filter. There were three
Varsity on his tail. The closest was only two yards behind
Will. He was screwed, but a little part of him loved this. It was
just like old times.

He had to lose these kids and do it now, before he started
slowing down. Someone swatted the tail of his sweatshirt.
Will pushed himself to max out his speed. His lungs felt like
they were turning inside out. The skin on his back was tin-
gling in anticipation of the hand that would grab his arm and
drag him to the ground.

Will slammed through a set of all-black double doors into a
lightless hall. He waited for the metal slap of the doors hitting
the wall again when the Varsity guys ran through. Seconds
passed, but still no sound. Will turned back and slowed.

The three jocks were standing in the doorway. They were leaning on each other and on the door frame, catching their breath. Will stopped and fell against the nearest lockers. He tried to laugh at them, but he didn't have enough wind in him. He pointed at them and shook his finger as if to say *nice try.* They didn't react, and Will was slow to realize that they weren't looking at him. They were looking above him.

Will craned his head up. The ceiling had been trenched. There was a five-foot gap that ran down the middle of the ceiling, the length of the hall. It opened Will's hall up to the hall above it.

Black legs dangled down from the ledge. Blue hair above it. Will stopped breathing altogether. He looked to the Varsity guys on his level, in the doorway. They shook their heads at each other, turned, and walked away.

Will got ready to run again, but *whump*, a black figure dropped into the hall from above. Then, two more behind the first, then four, then eight, thudding onto the floor. Will turned on his heels to run the other way. A figure in black dropped down right in front of him. The ceiling lights flickered on a floor above, and the electric blue of the kid's hair shimmered from the new pale light.

"You look lost," the Freak said.

"I'm good," Will muttered.

Will looked beyond the Freak to the double doors where the Varsity guys had just been. If there was ever a time for

David to show up out of nowhere again, it would have been now.

The Freaks behind Will grabbed him. The one in front of him sucker punched him in the stomach. Will gasped and a spray of his spit flew up on the inside of his mask.

"Jackal!" they started to yell.

No. *Not Bobby.* He writhed in the Freaks' grip. *Anybody but him.*

Even though Will was scared for his life, that fear was drowned out by an even stronger emotion: raging annoyance. Bobby had to be the most irritating person in all of McKinley. No one could feel bad for themselves as well as Bobby. Self-pity was his religion. He reveled in his own anguish. Always pouting. Always scowling. Always trying to broadcast to the world through his cartoonish evil costumes that he was someone to be feared. And pitied. God forbid that you forgot to pity him. That really drove Bobby up the wall. Obviously he was suffering worse than you, because look at the black makeup around his eyes, look at how he slouched and brooded.

Bobby/Jackal emerged from a darkened classroom. He'd shaved his head and painted his face black. He looked like a burned mannequin. The Freaks all seemed very impressed by Bobby's latest look. They smiled wickedly and stared at Will as if they were expecting him to faint at the sight of their leader. Bobby wove his way through the Freaks.

"What is that?" he said, tilting his black head. "A parent?"

"You're never gonna believe it," the Freak in front of Will said.

The whites of Bobby's eyes encircled his corneas when he recognized Will.

Bobby smiled, and it looked like his mouth was full of blood. As he approached, Will could see it wasn't blood. Bobby had slathered his teeth with glossy red nail polish.

He'd also gotten kind of fat. Will remembered laughing with Gates at Bobby's list of desirables that he'd delivered to the Saints, to request from the parents. Almost everything he'd asked for had peanut butter in it—bulk packs of Reese's cups, jumbo boxes of peanut butter Puffins, jars of all-in-one PB&J. Black might have been slimming, but it didn't do much for Bobby's new double chin. It looked like he'd been doing his suffering on the couch with corn dogs.

"What the fuck? Didn't you get out?" Bobby said. "What kind of dumb prick would come walking back into McKinley?"

Bobby turned to the rest of his gang and started laughing. It was a screeching giggle, and he held his belly as he did it. The rest of the hallway joined in, but at least the others sounded normal. Bobby sounded like a dying eagle.

Bobby grabbed the cylinders on Will's mask and shook his whole head with them.

"What is this?" Bobby said. "This is supposed to keep you safe?"

Will jerked his head away, but other Freaks grabbed his head and cranked it back until he faced Bobby.

"I mean, anyone who wanted to could pull this thing right off you." Bobby stared at him in disbelief. "I knew you were a stupid moron, but this is a whole new level."

Bobby rapped his knuckles on Will's head.

"Anything in there?" he said.

Will wished he could spit on him.

"You are completely powerless," Bobby said. He licked his red teeth.

"You are completely fat," Will said.

Bobby's smile shrunk to a pinched frown, like a bomb exploding in reverse.

"Bring him home," Bobby said with a sneer, "I've always wanted a pet."

"Always wanted a cookie," Will said.

Bobby worked a finger under one of the rubber straps that secured Will's mask to his head. He slid his finger closer to the mask, coming dangerously close to lifting up the rubber by Will's temple. Bobby gently blew on Will's temple.

"Got any more jokes?"

Will shook his head. He wanted so badly to say something mean, but he had to get a hold of himself. This was real. He could die. Bobby was practically blowing death into his face.

He shut up, and the Freaks took him home. They kept a firm grip on his arms and never gave him a moment to make a break for it. They carried him through the halls, hands wedged under his armpits, the toes of his boots barely scraping the floor.

"What are the chances you'd end up my prisoner *after* you graduated?" Bobby said from behind him, as the Freaks pushed him down the hall. "Guess good things really do happen in McKinley."

This was bad. Very bad. Will and Bobby had always hated each other, but in the past Will had almost always gotten the better of Bobby. He'd stolen from Bobby, injured him in food drops, mocked him publicly, and had spread multiple rumors about him that had driven Bobby crazy. That Bobby had constant diarrhea and had to wear a cloth diaper under his pants. That he played with dolls. That he got an erection whenever he cried. Bobby had a lot to want payback for.

The Freaks shoved Will through an archway that had been smashed through a hall wall. Will had never ventured this deep into the Freak base. He'd stolen a TV from them, but it had been from one of the rooms on the outskirts of their territory. There were so many holes in the walls, and walls that had been completely destroyed, that Will was afraid the ceiling would cave in. The place was like a beehive. The Freaks' destructive power was something to marvel at.

The Freaks had laid claim to most of the A/V equipment early in the quarantine and Will was finally getting to see what they did with it. He was led through a room that glowed with blue light. Bedsheets hung from the ceiling all around the room at different angles to each other, with blue images projected on them by old overhead projectors and new digital ones. Fans on the floor made the sheets dance. Will saw a fluttering blue video of Bobby sacrificing a naked Freak girl with a ceremonial knife like it was a pagan ritual—you could tell the knife was painted cardboard. Wobbling blue images were everywhere. A microscopic image of blood cells, an old anatomical etching of a skinless man whose muscles were unraveling from his bones, a close-up photo of a bare breast blotched and speckled with scabs.

In the next room, they'd rubbed soot all over the walls and ceiling, nearly blacking them out, and had carved images of screaming skulls and smiling demons into the walls. The carvings revealed the white of the drywall's core, turning the room into a black-and-white nightmare factory. A blue-haired girl was piercing her boyfriend's nipple with a sharpened bobby pin. Some Freaks were applying ghoulish makeup to their faces. Others were competing with each other over who could slump the most tragically in their chair. An atonal Freak band banged on desks in the corner. The singer's voice sounded like a garbage disposal full of phlegm, and they all wore black T-shirts with the words *Old Pervert* written in dripped bleach.

They walked him into a lecture hall. There was a twelve-foot pentagram burned into the floor. The walls were lined with televisions, and they all played the same footage of a crackling fireplace, surrounding everyone in the hall with a rectangle of fire. It bathed the room and all the Freaks in a warm, sweet-potato-colored light. A projection screen on the far wall showed camcorder footage of an old food drop in which the Freaks were dominating. Based on the angle of the video, the kid that had shot it must have been watching from a third-floor classroom. He did play-by-play commentary like it was a baseball game, and he cheered when Freaks snatched more than the other gangs or won fights on the battlefield. Freaks sat in chairs and watched the video and chatted with each other.

Bobby and his crew led Will through the room, to a sectioned-off area near the screen. It was separated from the rest of the audience by chest-high walls made of classroom doors that had been nailed together. Inside was a cardboard couch with stuffed T-shirt pillows. Bobby pointed to a spot on the floor.

"Put him there," Bobby said. "On his back."

Will tried to stop them, but he was no match for their combined strength. They put knees on his shoulders and hands to pin him to the floor. Hands held his ankles.

Bobby kicked something around the area like he was fooling with a soccer ball. It skittered across the floor. A human skull. Will reminded himself that Bobby used to wear part of a bio lab plastic skeleton, and that it was probably from one of those. But it didn't have the creamy yellowy-white color of a plastic skeleton. And it didn't look plastic. It looked like bone. Teeth were missing from it. He could see some hair. Where did Bobby get a human skull? Whose skull was it?

Maybe it was one of the teachers, Will told himself. Or one of the seniors who had died before graduation was established. Maybe some bodies had to be moved for some reason. Bobby could have just found it. Just 'cause he had a skull didn't mean Bobby was the one who killed the person. Probably not.

Bobby sank into a wooden chair and stared at Will. He whistled and a wide-thighed Freak girl, holding a plastic grocery bag and dragging a folding chair, came plodding in. When she reached Bobby, she sat and pulled a bottle of ink, a rag, and a mechanical pencil from the bag. A needle extended out of the pencil's tip instead of lead. She laid the rag over her forearm and dipped the needle into the black ink. Will watched her fold Bobby's ear forward and saw that the back of his ear was unpainted. It was only then, Will realized, Bobby hadn't painted his head and face black. He'd tattooed them. His eyelids, his lips. Up into his nostrils. Dull black.

"That's a tattoo?"

Bobby smiled with a mouth full of glistening red teeth.

"Almost done," Bobby said.

"Why would you do that?"

"You'd never understand. This is who I am now."

Bobby was right, Will didn't understand. He'd always

thought Bobby was all show, and that deep down he was a scared little wimp. But this . . . blacking out your entire head . . . Bobby was permanently deleting his old self. That scared Will. Maybe Will had always been wrong about him, or maybe Bobby had been pushed too far and he'd finally snapped.

The girl tapped away at Bobby's folded ear with the inky needle. Bobby pulled sugar cubes from out of his pocket and started eating them like popcorn. Bobby smiled so wide at Will that he saw an inch of pink gums above his red teeth.

"Scared?" he asked.

Will shook his head on instinct.

Bobby burst out of his chair and rushed Will. Will writhed against the knees that riveted him to the floor. Bobby stopped short of him and raised his boot in the air to stomp down on the face shield of Will's mask. But his foot hung there without smashing down. Bobby placed it back on the floor, and snickered down at Will.

"You should be."

20

PROM WAS IN TWO HOURS. AND THEN HILARY

would only stay for two more. That included dancing, posing for pictures, and being crowned prom queen. Immediately after her coronation, she'd run to the quad to be lifted out. That was a total of four hours. She could last four hours.

The wads of toilet paper she had wedged up her nostrils to stop the bleeding were getting soaked. She'd have to replace them soon. The hallucinations had begun, but they were minor. She'd seen her fingers as dove wings, and the way her white feathers had wrapped around the gun was beautiful. Sometimes, when she'd close her eyes, she'd be in a motel room where her mother was sucking face with Sam on stained bedding, and they were tearing off each other's clothes. She'd open her eyes immediately to rid herself of the sight, but sometimes it would take a few seconds for her vision to kick in. Even after she was firmly back in reality, she could hear the slippery wet noises of their mouths smacking together.

Hilary lay on a bed. She'd made Varsity construct a platform for the bed that rested on the top three bleachers. From there, she could keep an eye on everyone in the gym at all times. She yawned and stretched her arms in the air. The gun was in her hand, and everyone in the gym was either looking at it, or making a point not to. She knew they all craved it. And someone would come for it eventually. But by the time one of those idiots worked up the courage, she'd be gone.

Even with the power of the gun, she may not have gotten away with all her demands if the girls of the school hadn't rallied behind the idea of a prom. Every boy who griped about the work it took to make the prom happen had at least three girls surround him and threaten him if he were to do anything to derail this for them.

The Geeks were finishing decorating the commons in her chosen theme: spring. She had a Geek boy, two Pretty Ones, and a Nerd girl going without sleep to make four dress options for her that she'd try on shortly. She'd tested out five different makeup artists from across the gangs, but had yet to find one who could do her face justice. There were still more showing up to the gym for the chance to get on her good side.

If there was no one worthy, she'd do it herself. She was already going to do her own hair, but that was because she didn't want anyone standing behind her. Makeup artists stood in front of her where she could shoot them. But a hair-stylist, behind her back, could slip a wire around her neck and strangle her to death, and all Hilary would be able to do was blow holes in the ceiling.

There would be no other weapons allowed other than her gun, and Varsity would be working security at the doors. The Nerds had the largest music library in the school, and they were doing their best to perfect the playlist that she'd already gone through with a red pen. Everything was happening according to schedule. There was no way in hell she was leaving high school without being prom queen.

The gym floor became a giant pool of rice pudding in front of her eyes. The feet of the Varsity boys and Pretty Ones were buried in pudding halfway up their shins, and each step pushed the pudding around, ruining the perfect, lake-like surface. Blood began to bubble up through the displaced pudding like crude oil.

Hilary shook her head. When she looked back at the gym floor it was wooden again, the mulch of bloody pudding was gone, and all shins were dry.

She rubbed her eyes. She could do this.

The bleachers began to vibrate with footsteps. Her eyes bent left to see Terry limping up the bleachers.

"Stop," she said.

"I'm sorry," he said and hunched like a whipped puppy. "It's just, Bobby is here to see you."

"Didn't I already tell him to get lost?"

"Yes, you did," Bobby said from the gym doors. He and a troupe of Freaks entered the gym, all of them shrouded in black. One even wore a black sheet over his head like a medieval executioner. Bobby's head was black as well, like the burned head of a match. He opened his mouth and his teeth were crimson.

"If you've come to ask me to prom again, the answer is still no, I am not picking my prom king until the dance," Hilary said.

"I've come bearing a gift in the hope that you reconsider," Bobby said with a flowery bow.

"Don't be a pain in my ass, loser. Get to the point."

Bobby moved toward the kid with the executioner's shroud. On closer inspection, Hilary realized the sheet didn't have eyeholes. Bobby pulled the black sheet off the kid's head. It was David's little brother in a gas mask.

"Will. He's all yours. Your own uninfected. No one else in the school has one," Bobby said.

"What would I want with an uninfected?"

"Nothing, you should let me go," Will said. Bobby kicked Will's knee, and he fell to the floor.

"Well, word is that he didn't come back alone. David's back as well. He's not dead, and he's in McKinley."

And just like that, the last puzzle piece finally plunked into place, and Hilary's vision of her prom was complete. Her old sweetheart from her innocent days, David, would be her beau. It was just so . . . perfect.

"I'm certain he'd want to come to wherever his little brother is," Bobby said. "I've adored you forever, Hilary. I hope this gift finally proves to you how deep my feelings run."

Hilary looked Bobby up and down with a judgmental glare that made most boys shrivel. Bobby may have been a sniveling weirdo, but he held her gaze.

"You can walk me in," Hilary said.

21

WHEN HE SAW THE SCARECROWS, DAVID HAD
known. Somewhere ahead was Gonzalo's old Scrap hideout.
Early in the quarantine, Gonzalo had taken up residence in
the third-floor senior lounge after most of the seniors had
died. He'd cobbled together scarecrows and placed them
throughout the hall leading to the lounge, to creep out anybody who was thinking about wandering down this dead end.
They'd done the trick. It appeared that no one had set foot in
this dusty hall in a long time.

David held Lucy's hand tight as they wove between the
haggard figures. A plumbing pipe armature kept each one
upright. The bodies were made out of clothes stuffed with
trash, and the stinking sentinels were arranged in a staggered zigzag down the narrow hall. Each had clumps of real,
white hair obscuring its featureless face. Once-wet toilet
paper, that had dried and wrinkled, covered the floor. The

crusty, weaving mini mountain ranges were stained with nauseous colors. Dry yellow puddles. Reddish brown splatters that might have been blood. The paper had been torn up in places by dark grimy footprints. Tufts, clippings, strands, and tangles of white hair were dried into the paper, and they crunched underfoot like winter grass. The place stank, the walls were upholstered in a thick fabric of dust as if there were flypaper underneath. All of it made you wonder what kind of monster would choose to live at the end of this path. And then you'd see gigantic Gonzalo with a fire ax clutched in his paws. And you wouldn't think past that. You'd turn and run for dear life.

It showed a side of his old friend that David had never had a chance to see. When Gonzalo made a gesture it was always big, but day to day, he'd never been generous with his emotions. This place, however, was entirely his creation. It was a glimpse inside his mind—when he'd been just a kid trapped in school who'd wanted to go home. Even the big guy had been scared at some point and these sculptures had been his protectors and his company. Gonzalo had joined up with David because he'd needed a family, and in the Loners he'd found it, and he'd found love with Sasha. That had been why all the Scraps converged on him that day on the quad, why they'd fled the safety of their own hiding places. They'd wanted a family too. He felt proud to have given them that, and grateful that they'd gotten him out of McKinley alive.

David glanced over at Lucy as they walked down the scarecrow hall. She looked like she'd been spit out of hell in her chopped-up, pale pink hair and her black tattered clothes. Her face had lost its delicate fullness, and her fingertips were as black as talons down to the first knuckles. Her body was lean and firm, like she'd been through boot camp. She walked hunched, eyes searching, every muscle tense, like she was expecting an attack at any time. It broke his heart to think of what she had faced in here alone. The girl he remembered, her feet had barely touched the ground. She used to cling to his arm and let him lead the way in situations like this. She'd been innocent then, and he'd remembered wanting to preserve that. He'd liked protecting her from the dark side of McKinley. How long had she waited for David to come back and make everything right before her innocence had eroded away and she'd become like everyone else in here? It made his eyes water. How much had she suffered, thinking that any minute David would step in and stop it, like he'd always managed to do for her in the past? He felt responsible for all of it.

"I'm sorry it took me so long to come back," David said to Lucy. "I should have come sooner."

They reached the end of the scarecrow army, and Lucy looked at him. Her mouth was open, as if she was struggling for the right answer.

"You're here now," she said.

He'd abandoned her, and she was still being polite to him, still treating him like a hero.

"I should've never gone fifty feet from the door outside," David said. "But I ran. I figured if I could get help but . . . if I'd just stayed, I could've found a way to—"

"Don't say that. It doesn't matter now."

"It does," David said, emotion balling up in his throat. "I can't make up for the shit you've had to go through alone. But I want you to know that I'm sorry I let you down."

Lucy stared at him.

"I . . . ," David said, but he was afraid of what he might say. Somehow, simply being near Lucy had conjured up feelings he didn't know he had. Since he'd found out that Lucy was pregnant, and that Will was the father, David had been trying to convince himself, more than ever, that Lucy didn't mean anything to him. He was failing.

"What?" she asked. "What were you going to say?"

There couldn't have been a worse time to complicate things with his emotions. Lucy'd had a miscarriage. Will still didn't know. And David didn't know what Will and Lucy had together. Maybe theirs was the truest love of all. He'd already intercepted Lucy once and stolen her from Will. Was he really about to do that to his own brother? Again? Why save Will's life only to crush his spirit afterward?

"David, talk to me."

David looked away, to the third-floor elevator doors. They'd have to get the doors open somehow and climb down the shaft, but it was the safest way to circumvent the mob that was looking for them.

"If Will's in the elevator," David said, "we'll head straight to the quad, and be out of here before you—"

The school's PA system crackled to life. It was a sound that he had come to hate. It made him tense up like he'd seen cop lights in his rearview. He looked up at the cracked speaker by the ceiling, and heard his ex-girlfriend. Anger coursed through him at the sound of her lilting voice. His mind flashed to the memory of her crouching over him, chopping her hand down, and plunging her dagger into his eye.

"The greatest event in school history starts in an hour," Hilary's amplified voice said. "I wanted to let all my guests know that there's been an addendum to the dress code. Gas masks are now permitted. I already know one boy who'll be wearing one. An old friend of mine named Will. I hear his brother is here too, and I'm saving a spot on my dance card for him."

David's breath rocketed in his ears. He looked at Lucy.

"Daaaaaaaaavid...," Hilary called. Her voice was breathy like she was drunk-dialing. "I miiiiiiiiiiiss you. Do you miss me? Do you remember when I held you after you found out your mom died? Remember how good it felt to be in my arms? Don't you want that again? Don't you want to be my king? Or would you rather see what your brother looks like without a gas mask?"

A chill rolled down his spine.

Hilary cleared her throat. "Sorry, that just slipped out. Anyway, what do you say, baby?" Her voice was innocent and girly. "Will you go to prom with me?"

Hilary giggled and the speaker went dead. David leaned against the elevator doors. His brain felt dim. His body was exhausted and starved for food.

"You can't trust her. You know this is a trap," Lucy said.

He took a deep breath and blew it out slow.

"I'm going."

"David, you can't. She'll kill you."

"She has Will."

"Then I'm going with you."

"Actually, I already asked someone."

She swatted him in the arm, with a half-cocked smile. "Shut up."

"Okay, you can go with me."

"But we can't walk right in."

"No," David said. "We're gonna need some help getting in there."

"From who?"

"Let's hope I still have some friends in this place."

22

LUCY FELT BAD FOR LEONARD. AS HE LED them through the auditorium, up onto the stage, into the wings, and to the dressing rooms, he never looked at David once. Leonard held one guilty hand over his swirled green sherbet hair. As Lucy remembered it, Leonard had been the first to bail on the Loners for another gang. When David was dead, that had seemed like a smart move. Now it apparently filled him with shame.

Leonard knocked on a door marked with a golden star.

"Come in," a voice said from the other side.

Leonard turned the handle and pushed the door open.

"Thanks, Leonard," David said, and placed a hand on his shoulder. Leonard whimpered as if he'd been scalded and ran away.

David stepped into the dressing room. A long counter, with chairs tucked underneath, ran the length of one wall. It was swallowed up into a labyrinth of rolling racks, overstuffed with hanging costumes. Running above the counter was a row of individual mirrors, each framed by dead, gray bulbs. Each, but one.

Blazing lightbulbs outlined the square, central mirror where Zachary sat with his back to them, lit up like an explosion. He wore a suit jacket and pants that had been painted blaze orange and had orange feathers spraying out from the shoulders. The jacket didn't have a tail. It had a train like a bridal gown, covered in feathers transitioning from orange to red. He leaned toward the mirror with his eyes wide, putting the finishing touches on his makeup. Lucy watched his reflection as he stretched his face to apply his eyeliner.

"Back from the dead. Hell of a way to make an entrance. I always said you had a flair for the dramatic, didn't I, Davey?"

"It was all for your benefit."

Lucy's opinion of Zachary hadn't changed. She didn't like him and she definitely didn't trust him. It went all the way back to when he'd held a knife to David's throat and had tried to trade him to Sam. Somehow, David had forgotten about that. Or he'd forgiven it. Lucy wasn't good that way.

"If you're back in here," Zachary said, still focused on his own face, "it must be shit outside."

"You're not so far off," David said.

Zachary gave a little, self-satisfied grunt.

"Zachary, I need your help."

Zachary glanced through the mirror at them for the first time and sighed. He put down his eye pencil and began to powder a puff. "It's been a long day, David," he said, then raised an eyebrow. "Honestly, it's been a long couple of years."

"Tell me about it," David said.

Zachary scoffed. "Oh, please. Don't act like you know. You're only a legend because you burned bright and fast and disappeared. Try staying on top of a gang for as long as I have. I make it look so good that nobody even notices. That's what takes real talent."

Zachary patted down his face with the puff, sending little poofs of powder into the air like smoke signals.

"I believe it," David said.

"Mmm-hmm," Zachary said, unfazed. "So, what do you want?"

"We need to get into prom," Lucy said. "Varsity's going to be looking out for David. And I've got the Saints gunning for me."

"We need to get my brother," David said, "and get out of the school before we run out of air."

A smile curled Zachary's black-painted lips for the first time, and he turned away from the mirror to face them. He studied David, then Lucy, up and down, taking his time.

"I thought you two were lovebirds."

Lucy looked up to David. His mouth was open as if he were about to say something, but no words were coming.

"If you want to say something, Zachary, just spit it out already," Lucy said. "We don't have time for—"

"Whoa, whoa," Zachary said. "Easy does it, sister. I'm just trying to get the lay of the land. That's all. So, tell me if I'm wrong. Batman just reappeared in your life, and you can leave now, *but* you're going to give all that up, probably get him killed, just so you can make things weird again with Robin?"

Lucy felt nauseous.

"Oh, I'm sorry. Does Batman know about Robin?"

Now it was Lucy whose voice was stuck in her throat. She was having one of those clenching moments, when you're suddenly aware of everything at once, and how far things are from being okay. Lucy thought about Will for the first time, really thought about him. She knew he loved her, and she knew that kind of love didn't magically vanish just because her heart wanted something else.

"I know what happened," David said. "It doesn't matter. I need to save my brother."

Zachary clapped his hands and stood. He looked tickled.

"Well, this I've gotta see. This is the real show. Way more fun than a spoiled brat with a gun. Can you believe she gave me twenty-four hours to transform the commons? Everybody always wants top quality but they never want to wait for it. Naturally, I made miracles happen. She's lucky I'm a professional."

"You mean, she's lucky she has a gun," David said.

"That too."

"So, we're good? You'll sneak us in?"

"Yes."

Zachary spun on his heels and walked away from them, quickly vanishing behind the dense walls of costumes.

"Uh . . . ," Lucy said, trading looks with David. "We need to go. Now."

"You're not going anywhere with me, dressed like that," Zachary called out.

Hot water scalded the back of Lucy's neck but it felt good. The heat seeped into her muscles. She soaped up a lather and gently washed the cuts she'd gotten from her fall. Looking down her body at all the damage, she recognized something positive for the first time—she was lucky to be alive.

She closed her eyes and enjoyed the warmth washing over her skin. When Zachary had gotten up close to Lucy, he'd called her "foul" and insisted that she use his private shower to clean herself up before he loaned her anything from the Geek's huge supply of costumes. She didn't refuse.

Lucy pressed her hands to her face. Everything was crazy. If she and David lived through this, she'd still have to tell Will about the baby. And about her feelings for David. Will was probably going to hate her forever.

Life refused to get any easier.

Lucy laughed. Then groaned from an ache in her side, and

laughed again. She was going to her first prom. A dance, in a gown, with music from two years ago. Ridiculousness. She decided right then, right there, with thin streams of blood still running down her ribs, and her head still throbbing from a gasoline hangover, that she was going to try and enjoy it. Even if it was a pathetic excuse for a prom, it might be the only one she ever got, and it could be her last chance to enjoy anything.

Lucy finished cleaning herself and took a big breath before turning off the water. She dried herself off with a towel that felt so fluffy she wondered if it had ever been used. She wrapped it around her body and pushed open the bathroom door. Steam unfurled and sank when it hit the cool of the dressing room.

"What's the ETA on a shirt?" David said.

Lucy giggled and covered her mouth. David was standing in the middle of the room, bare chested with his gas mask on. His arms were outstretched with different outfits draped off them on hangers. Zachary parted a curtain of costumes and climbed through them, carrying a pink button-down shirt. He approached David and held the shirt up against his chest. With his free hand, he pressed the shirt to David's skin. Lingering. He tilted his head and leaned back, biting his lip.

"Mmm," Zachary said.

"What?" David said.

"Nope."

Zachary spun away from David and disappeared again among the clothes.

"We don't have all day!" David shouted after Zachary.

"Maybe you should've thought about that before you hit a tanning bed every day. Yours is not an easy skin tone to match, David!"

David looked to Lucy, who was still laughing.

"Do you know how many shirts he's tried on me already?" David said.

"I think he's enjoying himself," Lucy said.

David shook his head and let out a little laugh. "I should've listened to you. We could've been there by now."

"Maybe. Maybe not. Would it be weird to be excited about this?"

"What are you saying, you want to slow dance?"

Lucy grinned.

"Maybe."

David lifted his arms higher, inviting her to dance. All the outfits dangling from his arms swung, and a few fell off.

"Am I the date of your dreams?"

"Yep. I always had fantasies of making out with an astronaut stripper man. So, this is like the next best thing."

David started to writhe his hips like an exotic dancer.

"Is this doing anything for you?"

Lucy nodded. "Definitely. Whoof, how did Hilary ever let you slip through her fingers?"

"Well . . . ," David said, giving a grand finale hip thrust, "she dumped me."

Lucy cackled, then covered her mouth.

"Sorry."

"I think I'm over it."

"What was she like?" Lucy said. "I mean, if you liked her, and it sounds like she was there for you in a tough time, was she someone else then?"

David chewed on his lip.

"I used to think she was a nice person underneath," he said.

"Impossible. You dated Hilary 'cause you thought she was nice?"

"It was so long ago."

"That sounds like a cop-out."

"It's not a cop-out," David said, but he didn't seem to want to look in her eyes.

"Just admit it," Zachary said as he appeared with another shirt. "It was about the sex."

Lucy felt a cold swell of jealousy in her body. It was the answer she'd assumed but she was still surprised by how much she didn't want to hear it.

"She's a nice piece of ass. And so are you," Zachary went on. "Isn't that why narcissists get together?"

"Oh, is that what I am?"

Zachary held out a blue-and-white pinstripe shirt.

"I'm thinking classic, with a skinny black tie. Put that other stuff down," Zachary said.

David let the clothes drop, and Zachary held out one sleeve for David to slip into. "Now, button that up and tuck it in."

"Was it really about the sex?" Lucy said. She couldn't help herself, it slipped out.

David looked taken aback. He held her gaze as he put on the shirt. "Okay, I mean, yes, Hilary and I were good together that way. But that was back when everything was normal. We were dating. I don't know what you want from me." David threw his hands up, aggravated.

Lucy liked it that he pushed back and got frustrated with her. She couldn't boss him around.

"Nothing wrong with having chemistry," Lucy said, and smiled. She pulled the towel tighter around her body. "You can't help what your body wants." David smiled back, and he blushed.

It was nice to know she still had control over him in some ways. She felt more confident around him now than back in the Loners. She wasn't just some swooning freshman anymore.

"You know all about being powerless to what your body wants, right, Lucy?" Zachary interrupted.

"Excuse me?" Lucy said.

"Remember that Geek show?"

Lucy looked at him, confused.

"Who was that boy you were riding in the front row in the middle of my best performance . . . ever?"

"Riding?" David said.

"It wasn't Will," Zachary said, pretending to muse. "It was somebody else you were all over . . . couldn't keep your tongue out of him. Oh, right. It was that Nerd—Bart."

David was looking to Lucy for an explanation. She didn't know how to explain Bart without sounding like a real mess. Lucy glared at Zachary but he shrugged innocently.

"Nobody ever upstages me and gets away with it," he whispered. "I thought you knew that already, doll."

Lucy didn't let her face even flicker.

"Where's my dress?"

"Go nuts," Zachary said and flicked his finger in the direction of the costumes.

Lucy didn't look at David before she entered the costume maze. If she didn't answer Zachary's question, maybe David would forget. But as she tried on dress after dress, she worried that all the things she'd done in the past might not be so easy to shake. David might not want a future with her. She had to steel herself for that.

"Okay, time's up," Zachary called out to her. "We don't have all day."

Lucy rolled her eyes and pushed a path through the hanging costumes until she stumbled out into the area where

David and Zachary were sitting. They stared at her in the pink dress she'd put on. The satiny fabric held her tightly, like the unopened bud of a rose. Lucy had picked it because it matched the faded pink of her hair.

"What's wrong?" Lucy said.

David stood up. Zachary had worked magic. His blue suit looked tailor-made. Zachary had even dusted his gas mask with glitter.

"You . . . ," he said.

"Damn it!" Zachary said.

"What?"

"I really wanted to make fun of how ugly you looked, because let's be honest, when you walked in, you looked like a raccoon that'd been scraped off the bottom of a car, but now . . ."

"You look amazing," David said.

"She does!" Zachary said. He jumped up, ran over, and gave her a spin. "Ugh, I couldn't have done better."

"Really?"

"Really. I like. I wish I'd picked it out first," he said. "Oh, I wish I had your skin. You don't need anything. Except maybe . . ." Zachary looked around. He snatched up a tube of lipstick off the counter. "A pop of raspberry."

Before Lucy could even poke out her lips, Zachary was smearing her with lipstick. He gave her a little push toward David. David couldn't take his eyes off her.

"Look, about Bart. He was just this guy who—"

"It's none of my business."

Lucy smiled. "Thanks."

"I'm not a narcissist, by the way."

"I wouldn't blame you if you were. You look pretty good right now."

David laughed. He took her arm and looped it through his.

"As long as we're looking sharp, that's all that matters," David said as they began to walk out of the dressing room, arm in arm.

"This is going to be hell," Lucy said.

"I know."

HILARY LED WILL ON A LEASH. IT WAS A
nylon cord from a set of window blinds that Hilary had
bleached until it was bright white. She'd made a Varsity loop
it around Will's neck, tight enough to change the color of his
face. She held it with a delicate grip. Naturally, it matched her
white dress. All other girls had been forbidden from wearing
white at the prom. She'd spread the word in one of her prom
announcements: Show up in a white dress and you'll leave in
a red one.

Hilary held the gun close, so Bobby, four feet to her right,
or the Pretty Ones, ten feet behind her, couldn't make a grab
for it. It was a shame the gun wasn't white. If she'd had the
time to let it dry, she would have painted the thing to match
her dress too. Come to think of it, she should have painted
Will white, mask and all. Then he really would have looked
like her dog.

She only thought it, and then it was. Will's heavy breathing became tongue-lolling panting, and he was a white dog at her side. She laughed. So many of her hallucinations had been annoying, but this one she liked.

"Who would have thought, you and me going to prom," Bobby said.

"You're not my date, Freak," she said, and looked over at him. "You're my escort . . ."

Hilary lost her breath when she saw Bobby. He was as dejected as she thought he'd be, but the idiotic black stain that had covered his head was gone. Bobby looked like he used to look, before the quarantine. Baby blue polo shirt, floppy blond hair, and a backpack worn high and tight. She'd forgotten how preppy he used to be. Catalog perfect.

The entire hallway transformed. It sparkled like it had on the first day of school. The floor shined. The paint on the lockers was fresh. Every ceiling light worked and the hallway was bright as day from one end to the other.

She looked back at the people in her wake who had been commanded to keep their distance—the Freaks and the Pretty Ones and Varsity. They filled the hall, but their blue and yellow hair was gone. Instead, she saw natural hair color, of every variety. Every outfit looked fresh and new like they'd just been to the mall with their parents' credit cards. It was a new year, and everyone wanted to make a big first impression. Hilary was thrown off by the innocence of their faces.

They still had their baby chub. Their eyes were naive and unguarded. Some of them were girls who hadn't left her side in years, and she barely recognized them.

"Ready for your grand entrance?" Bobby said.

He stood at the closed double doors to the commons, ready to pull them open for her. The prom waited for her on the other side. Bobby was sparkling. She was waiting for her hallucination to break, but it didn't. She wondered if maybe she'd gone too far down the rabbit hole. Maybe she should skip her prom and head straight to the quad to be lifted out.

But what a waste of a dress. What a waste of an updo. Of a precision makeup job. Of an opportunity to be the most important girl in the world.

"Open the doors," she said.

As the doors opened, she forgot her worry. Springtime's colors flooded her eyes. Where the commons should have been, was a meadow in bloom. A gust of wind blew a cloud of flower petals, leaves, and pollen spinning past her. The meadow's grass was silky and verdant and it swayed slowly, like sea grass. Thousand-year-old birch trees with wide trunks were spread across the meadow, and their high branches intertwined overhead, providing cover from the blazing sun. Dappled light shined down through the breaks in the branches and it made the grass glow lime green in spots, and made the tops of people's heads flare bright like they were catching fire.

Everyone was dressed worse than her. Every girl, in every gang, had inferior hair. Their makeup either tried too hard or not enough. They were all riddled with flaws. Fat upper arms, premature wrinkles, acne, enormous thighs, lopsided tits, no tits, weak chins, hook noses, beady eyes, huge foreheads, low foreheads, hairy arms, cavewoman eyebrows, tacky nails, recycled dresses, dirty sneakers, stubby fingers, girl mustaches, blubber asses.

This was heaven.

She switched her focus to the boys. Their clothes were all stupid but she didn't care. What mattered was the way they were looking at her. Some smoldered. They wanted to ravage her body. The others had pleading, helpless eyes that told her they knew they'd never be good enough for her. Both reactions were wonderful, and together it was like a chocolate vanilla swirl of soft-serve.

A gathering wind ruffled her dress. Leaves began to blow off the trees and get caught in the vortex of wind circling the meadow. The vortex spun slowly all around them. Hilary and the others were standing in the eye of a lazy hurricane. A light flashed in the corner of her eye. There for an instant and then gone. She saw another flash. A sparkle.

There were mirrors flying through the air. First just a few, then there were a hundred. No matter where the mirrors were in the hurricane wind, they were facing her at all times. A hundred reflections of Hilary. From every angle, from every height, she was perfection. There was no point of view from which she looked bad. It wasn't possible.

She tugged on Will's leash. It was time to dance. With the first swing of her hips, the mirrors shattered to dust. The music came blasting in. She pointed her gun out in front of her and spun, so everyone would know to give her space. The other kids backed up without question, and the center of the grassy dance floor was hers.

Hilary knew how to move. She based all of her dance moves on the positions that showed off her features the best. She simply transitioned between her favorite poses to the beat. Every slight movement was a gift to her audience, allowing them to see a new aspect of her precious form. She hoped they were grateful for the chance to look at her, to be moved by her grace, by her limitless beauty. *They should be happy . . . because I am happy.* She knew that the light that she had inside was shining on them now, and they all felt it. They'd remember this night forever.

They watched her, encircled her, but didn't dare to come close. Soon she could see nothing but their eyes. The mirrors, and the meadow, and the wind faded away until there were only eyes. Jealous eyes. Heartbroken eyes. Awestruck eyes. Then, she could no longer see their expressions. They became disembodied eyeballs, floating at head height. Wet Ping-Pong balls with capillaries and corneas. More eyeballs popped into existence. So many that the eyeballs crammed in close to each other to get a look. More and more appeared, until they were so densely packed together that they formed a dome over her, like she was nestled inside a giant igloo, and they stared and stared and stared.

It was, without a doubt, the greatest moment of Hilary's life.

IT WAS CRAMPED IN THE BOTTOM OF THE
rolling drink cart, but that was the least of their problems.
David was scrunched up into a ball, and so was Lucy, right
in front of him. They sat kneecap to kneecap, hugging themselves. A white tablecloth was draped over all four sides of
the cart, keeping them hidden. The cart's wheels rumbled
along the dirty floor. Light that came through the white cloth
surged and waned as they were rolled past functional ceiling
lights.

"Should we look?" Lucy said.

"Better wait for Zachary to give us the cue," David said.

He wanted to look though. It was killing him not to. The
closer he got to the commons, and the closer he was to facing
Hilary. He was getting scared.

The cart came to a stop. Zachary lifted the tablecloth and
crouched at their level. His gold-dusted hair arced off his

head in tendrils and dangled like the branches of a willow tree.

"This is where we say good-bye," Zachary said. "I will not be making my entrance with a drink cart, thank you very much. I'll enter first, so that all eyes will be on me when you get pushed in. The cart will be left somewhere safe. When it stops moving, it's time to get out."

"All right. Thanks for doing this Zachary. I can't tell you how much it means," David said.

"It means about seven blow jobs by my estimation."

"You never change."

"I prefer the morning. A week of wake and blows."

David shook his head. His smile faded. He took a deep breath. "If I don't see you again, I hope things work out for you."

Zachary ogled him, dumbfounded, then looked around and made sure no one was listening.

"You're a good person, David. I'm sorry I tried to kidnap you that time."

Zachary extended his hand, and David shook it.

"Uh, it's okay. I like you too."

Zachary let go and gave his eyes a quick wipe.

"Shit, you're making me mess up my makeup."

Zachary whipped the tablecloth back down.

"Good luck, honey thighs. Cannot wait to see what you do to Hilary," Zachary declared through the cloth.

"Me neither," David said with an empty chuckle.

They listened to the footsteps of Zachary and his entourage as they walked away from the cart. David could barely hear Zachary proclaim, "I'm here!" in the distance.

"What *are* you going to do?" Lucy said.

He looked at her. Her face was nearly pressed against his face shield. Her eyes were wide open and jittery.

"Smooth-talk her?" David said.

"Please tell me you're joking," Lucy said.

The cart started to move. They were on their way.

"I just need to get close to her. When I have her off guard, that's when I'll grab the gun. Don't worry," David said.

But he was worried. He was getting more worried the more he thought about it. The cart paused, and he could hear the low voice of what he assumed was one of the Varsity guards. David wondered if he knew the guy, and what he would do if he discovered them. He heard the Varsity guard say, "Have fun," then the cart started rolling again.

It was too quiet. He'd expected to hear people partying in the commons. The shouts of a big crowd. Instead, what he heard was a low murmur, drowned out by a blaring pop ballad. David almost knew it by heart from the countless times Hilary used to play it in her car. It was an insufferable song called "Ask Myself Out" where the singer sang about how they look so hot, they're about to ask themselves out. The refrain, *Ask myself out, ask myself out, lookin' so good gonna ask myself out,* repeated for six minutes.

The refreshment cart came to a stop. He stared into Lucy's eyes and wished that he could do anything but get out from under that tablecloth.

"Is it time?" Lucy said.

"Yep, let's go," he said, assuming a brave tone. He slipped his head out and saw that the cart was in the shadow of one of the thick cement columns of the commons, and that no one was around. He got out and Lucy followed. She had her hands on his back, and he could feel her looking over his shoulder as he edged into the light and peered around the side of the column.

The two-story room had been transformed. Bark textures and knotholes had been drawn on the wide concrete columns that held up the second-floor balcony, to make them look like massive birch tree trunks. Geeks were at strategic spots throughout the room, agitating glass jars full of apple juice and chicken bouillon cubes in front of robust stage lights taken from the auditor-ium. The light that shined through the sloshing liquid lapped at the ceiling and walls, its golden brown light undulating, the colors of lemons and honey and molasses. The entire underside of the balcony was covered in paper leaves, cut from college-ruled three-ring binder paper. More light was projected up through lime-flavored Gatorade in jars, drenching the leaves in green. The place was stunning. Zachary had outdone himself.

David studied the crowd. Most of the school was here,

whether they wanted to be or not. This was where the action was. A chance to get ahold of the most powerful object in school. A chance to see some blood spilled. He hoped that there were some kids here who only wanted to dance. A lot of boys wore a basic "tux" of dyed-black pants and white T-shirts with buttons glued down in a line. Each T-shirt had a cardboard collar with a black paper shape of a bow tie glued to the front. Girls wore toilet paper corsages. The toilet paper squares had been folded into petal shapes and curled, then stitched together into blooming paper blossoms. Some girls had new dresses, but most wore old ones with a little bit of extra effort put in, like a satin bow in their hair, or homemade high heels. One girl wore a ruffled poodle skirt that had been stuffed with pink insulation fluff. It shouldn't have been a surprise to David, after having Zachary as their personal dresser, but he and Lucy looked overdressed.

And then there was always the matter of the gas mask on his head. There was no blending in. Whatever plan of action he was going to take would have to be swift. His recycled breath blew heavy in his ear. It was getting harder to breathe.

He gave Lucy's hand a squeeze. "Have a look around and see if you can find where she has Will. I'll handle Hilary."

"I don't have a good feeling about this, David."

"When I get the gun," he said, as if he hadn't heard her, "we'll leave out that exit over there and go straight to the quad. I don't think we'll be able to run and keep everyone at bay. But

I'll watch the crowd if you and Will look out for ambushes."

Lucy nodded, her bottom lip wobbling.

"I'll see you in a minute," he said.

"Okay," Lucy said, her voice cracking apart. She squeezed his hand back so hard it hurt. "Last time I said good-bye to you . . . you died."

"That isn't going to happen," he said. He hoped he was right.

"You make sure. You hear me?"

"I will."

They embraced, and when they let go, she walked away. She only looked back once and her face was pinched with tension like she was trying not to cry. Lucy headed toward the west wall, keeping to the shadowed areas. Whenever she stepped into the light, it would make her dress glow a shimmering pink, and catch the fine pink lines of her body. She disappeared around the curved staircase to the second floor. He hoped that wouldn't be the last time he saw her.

The music shifted nicely from Hilary's ballad into a dance track, but the crowd in front of him didn't respond. A few swung their bodies to the bass beat, but most people were staring at the dance floor. David got closer. People were packed in close together, except for a twenty-foot circle of clear floor in the center, where Hilary danced by herself. A spotlight followed her. She held the silver revolver over her head and it shined so brightly in the spotlight's beam that David had to squint. Hilary started to spin in a circle, laughing, with her arms outstretched like she was spinning gleefully through a field. The gun was leveled at the crowd's heads now. Gasps rippled through the crowd as they ducked.

David pushed forward. As he cut through the crowd, he could feel eyes turning and sticking to him. His presence in the school had been announced over the PA. He was expected by the crowd. He was the next big twist in the psycho soap opera that was playing out in front of them. He could hear their whispers. It was all so familiar. Like the last seven months hadn't passed at all. They stepped out of his way, made a path. Some cheered him on and laughed at the sheer craziness of it all.

David stepped into the circle. Ten feet ahead was Hilary. She danced completely off beat from the music, like there was a different song in her head. She smiled at the crowd like they were smiling back. They weren't. Even the Varsity and Pretty One couples stared at her as if she was bonkers. David kept his eye on the gleaming gun. So did everyone else.

He walked toward her. She was beautiful, even more beautiful than normal. She had a special radiance to her, because she was happy. He could barely remember her brimming with this much life, this lost in the moment. It was a lie, he told himself. She split your eyeball like a soft-boiled egg. She'd mutilated him. Every time he looked in a mirror, he had to think of her. He'd never be rid of her.

Hilary saw him approach. Her face lit up and she squealed.

David felt a familiar feeling inside, one he wished he could have suppressed. A yearning for Hilary. This wasn't the first time he'd felt it, against his better judgment. When he had seen her in the halls as the leader of the Pretty Ones and he had been a Scrap, he'd been filled with anger that she had slept with Sam and dumped him. But later, he would fantasize about her. In the fantasies, it was always in his bedroom in his family's house, like they used to do before the quarantine. She was a touchstone to the life he'd had before. Eventually she'd cheated on him, dumped him, stabbed his eye out and all the rest, but before all that, life had been good. They'd been a popular couple. He'd been killing it on the football field; and his mother had been alive. The future had been promising. That was a time he would never get back. Except sometimes, the sight of Hilary's face would bring him flashes of that old feeling, the safety of his old life, of his mother, and the trust he had in the world then. He wished it wouldn't.

"Take forever!" Hilary said. She waved him forward in a cartoonish manner. "Oh my God, how are you?" she asked.

David didn't know what game this was.

"Uh, I'm good, Hil. Considering . . . ," he said as he walked toward her.

"You look really cute," she said and then giggled and looked away. She usually wasn't the eyelash-fluttering type. At least, she hadn't been, not for a long time. Usually she looked at you straight with eyes like slits of ice. She had to be messing with him somehow, but he wasn't getting the joke.

"Got your message," David said as he reached her.

"How do I look?" she said, and pointed the gun at his head.

"Gorgeous," he managed to say, watching the barrel of the gun.

A giggle escaped her lips. Tears clustered in the corners of her eyes. They didn't seem like fake tears.

"I know," she squeaked.

She pulled him in close to slow dance. She put one hand around the back of his neck and pressed the gun against his temple with the other. David's insides were quaking. He felt the potential of the gun's blast on his temple. She was staring up at him with affection, a knowing smile on her face. He put his hands on her waist and she cooed. They rocked back and forth slowly, out of tempo with the fast song. The colored light seemed to swirl around them as they turned. She twisted her body and craned her neck around like she was savoring a delicious sensation in her body.

The longer they danced, the more uncomfortable he felt. He couldn't tell what she was really after here, but he had to find Will.

"About Will. I—"

"Do you remember the time you brought me to the creek?" Hilary said. She traced her finger down David's arm.

David nodded. It had been their first date.

"You always flirted with me in physics. And you were so cute. But you made me wait for two months before you asked me out. You jerk."

She playfully tapped the gun against his mask for emphasis.

"I guess you came off as intimidating," David said.

Hilary giggled again.

"That creek was so pretty. But it was so dorky that you brought a picnic. That was so . . . you."

She was flirting with him.

"But you made out with me anyway," David said. He added a cocky grin, and she grinned back.

"I almost didn't," she said. "You're lucky the date I had that night was a bomb, otherwise you never would have gotten a second chance."

"You went on a date with somebody after you went to the creek with me?"

"Caleb Miser, a senior. Turned out he was a loser too. Let's just say, once he got excited, he didn't know how to calm down."

David tensed. He didn't like this at all. To his horror, he was feeling jealous of Caleb Miser. It was just a little, but he was definitely feeling it. Like Hilary was still his girlfriend. He wanted to stomp out these feelings.

"Why are you telling me this?" he said.

She covered her mouth. "Oh my God, isn't it beautiful

here? Wouldn't this be the perfect place to get married?"

David's stomach did a back flip. "What?" he said.

"Married," she said. "Let's just do it. The two of us. Wouldn't it be wild? I used to think about it a lot back when we were together."

"Hilary, I . . ."

"Maybe you should get down on one knee."

David looked around at the crowd, watching them. Shuffling their feet. Their gaunt faces lit by tan and green light. Part of him was tempted to get down and propose, just to play along, and keep her talking until he could make a grab for the gun, but his pride wouldn't let him. Her brow furrowed when he stayed upright.

"I'll say yes, silly, you don't have to worry about that," she said. "I'll marry you, David Thorpe!" she shouted to the room. Her smile was ecstatic. "Right here on the beach, under the sun."

He studied her face. Her eyes darted around like everything was catching her attention at once. He looked closer at the dark crust inside her right nostril. Dried blood. She was in the final stages of transitioning. David remembered the chaos of being in that state, where memories, fantasies, and nightmares ebbed and flowed over the shores of reality.

"Hilary, you have to get out of here. Fast. I can help you. But I need the gun," David said. His tone was sharp, but he needed to cut through her hallucinations.

Hilary jolted from his words. For a moment, she looked scared. Her gaze danced across the surrounding crowd. She began to withdraw the gun from David's head, and he reached one hand up to take it. Hilary swatted his hand back down and cracked the gun against his face plate again.

"You'd like that, wouldn't you, Sam?"

David stayed still. He tried to keep his voice gentle. "I'm not Sam," David said. "You're seeing things, Hil."

She shook her head. Her trigger finger twitched.

"No, you're jealous, 'cause you lost Varsity and now they're mine. This whole school belongs to me. And if you want a piece of it, you better get on your knees and start kissing my feet!"

Hilary had David down on his knees. Whatever he had just said had really pissed her off, and Lucy was beginning to realize that getting David and Will out of school alive might come down to her. It was an awful thought.

She was going to fuck it all up, just like she'd fucked up everything in her life since the moment she'd decided to stab Gates.

She looked across the commons from her hideout. She had tucked herself into the fold of one of the stage curtains that the Geeks had hung to create a storage space hidden under the staircase. Lucy locked her sight on Will, who sat on the floor with his hands secured behind his back. His masked head was bowed in shame. A white leash led from his neck up to the blackened hand of Bobby, who stood beside him, amid a mixture of Freaks and Varsity, watching the action on the dance floor. Lucy felt a surge of emotion, seeing Will again. She hated seeing him humiliated. She couldn't deny that her feelings for him were strong. They'd been through so much together. They'd lost their virginity to each other. Everything came back to her in a rush. The snuggled-up morning after in the plant room. She saw him telling her he loved her under the deep red lights of the Slut lounge. She saw him lifting away from her as the raindrops splashed on her face. She felt the ache of their last kiss being stolen from them by the tug of the crane.

A hand reached out from behind Lucy, grasped her over her mouth, and pulled her back through the curtains, into darkness. The music became muffled. A thin wheezing breath replaced it. Lucy tried to scream, but her captor's grip was tight.

"I saved you," said a crackly, Southern voice.

Lucy turned, and the hand let her go. Bile stared back at her. He wore a glow-stick necklace that made his spectral face look as if it were floating in the blackness.

"Why'd you run away?" he said.

"I . . . I had to go."

"Go where?"

"With my friends."

"But I'm your friend."

"I know that, but we only just met. These friends are . . . everything I have."

"But . . . I love you."

"You don't," Lucy said. "You just think you do."

"I LOVE YOU," Bile said and thrust his face into hers. His mouth was pocked with sores. His breath was salty and bitter like his insides were rotting.

"Well, I don't love you," Lucy snapped back.

Bile shrunk away from Lucy. He looked frightened of her, and for some reason, that only made her more upset.

"What do you think we would do, Bile? Go back to your place and get high? Forever?" she said, her temper flaring.

"M-my name's Kyle," he said.

She sighed when she saw how much her anger was hurting him. "I can't live like you do," she said, "wishing you were dead or whatever you're doing to yourself. You don't deserve it."

Bile's eyes welled with tears.

"I don't deserve it either. I want a happy life. I'm sick of being afraid all the time. Of hiding. I don't want to do that anymore. I'm going out there, and somehow I'm going to get that gun, and then I'll leave this shithole once and for—"

Bile pushed Lucy out of his way, whipped a curtain aside, and was gone.

Lucy stared at the curtain, slowly closing. She stuck one hand out to stop it, and stepped through, back into the commons. People were shouting. A few were on the floor. They'd been pushed by Bile as he muscled through the crowd.

"Bile!" Lucy let slip.

She jumped over a fallen Skater and hurried through the field of bodies. When she reached the empty dance floor, David had been knocked down and was trying to get his footing. Bile was grappling with Hilary, who was screaming at the top of her lungs. The gun swung 'round, still in Hilary's hands, but with Bile's fingers working their way under them. Kids in the crowd hit the deck. Lucy lurched to a stop when the barrel's path crossed hers. Bile stomped Hilary's foot, and the couple fell to the ground.

A cracking *BOOM* punched the air. Bile and Hilary stopped moving. No one in the commons moved. A sweet harmony crested out of the sound system. Bile pushed off Hilary, who lay still on the floor. He stood and turned. He clutched the pistol in his right hand. Smoke slithered from the gun's nose. He raised it for the crowd to recognize and fear. They stayed frozen.

Bile's other hand was on his belly. Red spilled over his fingers and down the back of his hand. He was covering a gurgling hole. He stepped toward Lucy and stumbled.

"Oh no," she whispered.

He lumbered toward her, walking a drunken zigzag until he was only a foot away.

"You shouldn't be afraid," Bile said.

He placed the bloody gun in her hand, and dropped.

His breathing stopped. The blood puddle spread underneath him. He'd died so she'd have a chance to live. Or he had killed himself. Or both. It was too much to bear. She felt like the room was closing in on her. But it wasn't the room. It was the circle of people around her, closing in, step by tentative step.

Lucy looked to the gun in her hand. Bile's blood made it slip as she squeezed her fingers around it. She held the gun up, just as Hilary and Bile had done before her. It seemed to press pause on the crowd's advance.

"Back up!" Lucy shouted.

"We have to get out of here," David said from somewhere in her periphery.

She breathed for the first time at the sound of his voice. She moved toward him, keeping her eyes nimble.

"Bobby!" David said. "Let my brother go."

Bobby dropped Will's leash and put his hands up. Will wasted no time standing and running over to them.

"Hi," Will said. He smiled at Lucy like nothing else existed.

That smile that said *fuck the world*. It got her every time. This time it made her heart hurt.

"Hi," she said. She wanted to hug him tight, but instead she shouted at everybody else: "We're walking out of here."

Lucy kept her elbow locked and swung the gun across the crowd.

"You heard her," Will said. "She'll kill you, straight up. Try her. Go 'head and try her."

"Will, cool it," David whispered.

The threesome were quick to fall into a triangular formation, so they could watch all sides. Even though everyone was still a good ten feet away, it felt as though someone could still grab the gun. And with her hands still wet with blood, it could have slipped right out.

"Let's go," David said.

They began to move in sync toward the west exit, in the direction of the quad, but a low moan drew everyone's attention. Lucy looked over to see Hilary rising up from the floor. She was clutching her head. She looked around with fierce eyes. The fingers on her right hand moved furiously as they noticed that they were no longer in possession of the gun. They raised up and one extended to point directly at Lucy.

"You!" Hilary said. "That doesn't belong to you! Give it back!"

"Go to hell," Lucy said.

Hilary shook her head. "I wish you'd died when I pushed you off the stairs."

Lucy's feet froze. Will bumped into her.

"I think we should run," Will said.

He didn't know. He couldn't comprehend what Hilary meant. Lucy could barely believe what she was hearing. But David seemed to understand.

"Lucy, forget it," David said, and took her hand. "Come on."

She pulled her hand out of his.

"*You* pushed me?" Lucy said, stepping away from David and Will.

Hilary smiled. The truth of what Hilary had done lit a fire in Lucy. Her baby. Her and Will's baby. She hadn't lost their child. Hilary had taken it from her.

Lucy stomped right up to Hilary and put the gun to Hilary's head. Hilary's attitude crumbled as the gun's cold barrel dimpled her temple.

"Lucy!" David called out. "It's not worth it."

Lucy glanced over at David. He had both hands out like he was talking to a jumper on a ledge. Will looked confused.

"It is worth it! Do you know what she did?" Lucy said, then locked eyes with Hilary.

She could feel Hilary shiver. The crowd waited for what would happen next. David looked at her like she was a monster. Will shook his head back and forth fast. She put her focus back on the shivering bitch who had stolen her baby.

"Take it out," Lucy said.

"What?" Hilary said with a tremor in her voice.

"The tooth. Take it out now."

Hilary went pale as boiled chicken. She shook her head in a tight little movement. Lucy clicked the hammer back.

Hilary raised a shaking hand to her lips, then stopped.

"Please," Hilary said, her eyes pleading with Lucy.

"Do it," Lucy said.

Hilary clenched her eyes shut. She gripped her tooth between her thumb and knuckle. A tear squeezed out and ran down her cheek. She pulled. The commons gasped. Hilary covered her mouth with her hand.

"Hand down," Lucy said.

Hilary cried more, but she did it.

"Now, smile for everyone."

The tears poured out of Hilary. Lucy had never seen Hilary cry before. She sobbed as she spread her lips and displayed the gaping black hole in her perfect smile. A trickle of watery blood flowed down from the gum and across one of her front teeth, and then dripped onto her lower lip. Laughter rose in the room. Hurried whispers. No Pretty Ones came to her aid. Hundreds of sneaker soles squeaked across linoleum as the crowd packed in close together to get the best view. Flashes of light. At least a hundred cell phones were held in the air, freezing Hilary's shame forever in pictures and video.

"Your prom queen, everybody," Lucy said. "The leader of the Pretty Ones."

Hilary hyperventilated. She dropped to her knees, one arm on the ground, red drool spilling from her mouth.

"You're going to pay for this," she said. "I'm going to make you—"

A red, wet chunk leapt out of her mouth. It landed on the floor with a heavy splat. The whole room gasped. Hilary straightened, and both hands went to her throat. Blood barreled out of her mouth like floodwaters out of a storm drain. It splattered heavy onto the floor. When the blood stopped gushing from her, Hilary wobbled like a slowing top, then fell face-first into the red slop that was once her lungs.

25

DAVID HAD SEEN ENOUGH.

He rushed to Lucy's side, and so did Will. Lucy was smiling over the body of his dead ex-girlfriend, and he didn't like it. He didn't like any of it, not her happiness at seeing Hilary die, not the drooling crowd watching death like it was a sporting event.

David placed his hands over Lucy's. They were cold.

"Give it to me," David said.

The shaking tension in her hands relaxed. He took the gun from her.

"Make a path!" David shouted. "We're leaving!"

David swung the gun in a half circle at the crowd that was gaping at Hilary's wasted body. No one moved, but their eyes settled on the steel in his hand instead.

David thrust the gun in the direction of a pack of Skaters who stood in the way of the west exit.

"You wanna die? Huh?" Will said. "'Cause he'll make it happen!"

Shut up, Will. The crowd closed in on the trio.

"Get back!" Lucy shouted.

Kids crept forward, a mad hunger in their eyes. The circle closed tighter. They were never getting to the quad.

David realized what he had to do. Sam's dad had shared a plan with him, *a final solution,* he called it. It was only to be used as a last resort, and David hadn't told Will or Lucy about it, because he hadn't wanted anything to do with it. He didn't want to be responsible for more lives lost.

He cocked the hammer back.

Three kids ran at him.

David raised the gun and emptied it into the ceiling.

BLAM. BLAM. BLAM.

Everyone cowered and slid to a stop, covering their heads with their arms.

Click. Click.

He wanted them to hear that, and know the gun was useless now, like all the others in the school.

"Are you out of your mind?" Will said.

David ignored him, and tossed the gun into the crowd. A few scrambled for it, but most of the kids understood.

"This quarantine has gone on too long. None of you deserve to be locked up in here," David said.

"No shit!" someone yelled.

"Nobody wants to hear it, buddy boy," P-Nut said. "You just threw away the microphone." The leader of the Skaters sauntered forward from the crowd and smiled. "Skaters, the good times are back. I think we've found ourselves some hostages. Grab 'em!"

Skaters charged toward him.

"I know a way out!" David yelled.

The Skaters halted.

"You do?" Will said.

"A possible one," David said to the crowd. "Isn't that what you want, to walk out of here, once and for all?" He looked into the eyes of as many people as he could. Hope glinted there.

"It's time to leave. Things never should have gone this far. I'm not saying it's going to be a friendly world out there, but you should be free. You deserve the chance to deal with the situation yourselves, make your own choices, not tear each other apart in here. But, if we're gonna have even a chance of pulling this off..." They clung to his every word. "It's going to take every single one of us."

David's palms pressed against steel. He pushed. Lucy and Will flanked him, pushing hard, and the rest of the school stretched out on either side of him, all pushing on the steel wall in the back foyer. He remembered when this wall of steel plating used to be an inviting glass entryway that looked out to the faculty parking lot. The crowd grunted and strained.

The ones who couldn't fit pushed on the backs of the ones at the wall.

Behind them, the massive old mural that depicted David in front of the Loners, under a blue sky, loomed over the two-story foyer. The squares of butcher paper that illustrated the Loners had fallen away. What remained was most of David's face, and five small squares of blue, like an 8-bit sky.

David had told them about Sam's dad's final solution. A month back, when the school had been damaged by the grenade attack, and the steel plate that sealed up the back foyer had become detached, it had given Sam's dad an idea. If there was ever a need to evacuate the students inside, if something were threatening their lives, say a fire, they would need an evacuation route that could get the kids out quickly. The detached steel wall had been chosen as that exit. Its immense weight was doing the work of keeping it upright. In the event of a crisis, they'd pull the wall down with the crane, and the kids could escape to safety. A steel rivet had been driven into the concrete of the building to keep the wall attached. The whole school had to be stronger than a single rivet.

"Push harder!" David yelled.

This had to end. They had to be set free. He knew he'd be risking the lives of uninfected adults out there, but things had gotten too savage. It would be a mess having everyone outside, but there was no way to avoid it. This was a messy situation. On the farm, he'd believed the infected were safest inside the school, but he'd forgotten how sick McKinley was, and now he realized that its sickness was terminal. If David didn't get them out of this place, they'd destroy each other.

"Everyone work with me when I say *push!*" David shouted.

Hundreds of hands waited for his command.

"PUSH!" David said.

Everyone moved as a unit, shoving with everything they had in them.

"PUSH!"

He heard a pop of metal. The wall jolted forward. A two-inch-wide line of daylight appeared above them, where the plates met the building. A whistling alarm rang out from the outside.

"Keep pushing!" David said.

The crowd pushed harder and the metal creaked. He heard Varsity snarl with effort, he heard the higher-pitched grunts of girls, giving their everything. He saw Skaters piling in with Freaks, Nerds with Geeks, Saints with Sluts, working together, refusing to quit.

Another pop sounded out. Then a few more. The stripe of daylight above them widened, and David felt the wall begin to pull away from his hands. It tipped in what seemed like slow motion at first, then it sped up. He couldn't help but fall forward with the welded plates, like everyone else. Clouds of dry dirt whooshed into the air as the metal wall hit the ground with a reverberating crash. Daylight flooded the foyer. David had to shut his eye from the sting of the light.

When he opened his eye, he saw the farm in all its glory. Moist, freshly tilled soil. Lush green grass. He saw a wheelbarrow full of ripe heirloom tomatoes. The sky was crowded with cotton ball clouds, each rimmed with golden light. Snow-frosted mountains seemed a million miles away. Cows lumbered away from the noise of the wall's crash. Goats bleated in protest. Three dogs scampered into view, chasing each other.

He saw the parents. They were clustered together by the compost bins, a hundred feet away, all wearing gas masks or breathing through scuba gear, and they looked nervous. The whistling alarm blared continuously.

The line of McKinley kids stood breathless at the threshold to freedom.

"Mom?" David heard someone say.

Bobby walked out onto the fallen steel wall. Bobby's mother broke away from the other parents and burst forward.

"Bobby! Baby, come here," she said.

Bobby sped forward. When they got up to each other, she slowed to a stop. She cocked her head and took in his dull blacked-out skin, his shiny red teeth. Bobby stopped a few feet short of her, trembling, and they stared at each other. The alarm whistled. A gentle wind blew the rich scents of a farm into the foyer.

Bobby's mother opened her arms to him and they embraced. The hug was like a starter pistol. Everyone sprinted out of the school after that. David ran with them. It was madness, so many people running in different directions. He lost track of Lucy and Will. His old friends and enemies were all around him, smiling, and running in circles. They leapt through the crops, playing. They ran with arms outstretched, kicking up dirt, spreading themselves across the expanse of the thriving farm like it was the first minute of recess. They leapt, they embraced, happy faces glistened with tears. Only a few hesitant ones remained in the commons, slowly inching out, wary of their own liberty.

Parents were reuniting with their children everywhere he looked. Terry's parents came up to thank David for giving them back their son. He saw Sam's father off in the distance, running around like a madman, trying to wrangle all of the kids.

Lucy ran up to him. The look she gave him threw David. He had been looked at like that before, but never by Lucy. It was how Hilary used to look at him when she'd jumped into his arms after winning a football game. It was how girls used to look at him at parties when they wanted to steal him from Hilary. It was aggressive. Charged with desire. She threw her arms around him. David forgot the rest of the world around him. She kissed his neck. He closed his eye. He melted into her.

"That was amazing," she said.

Kiss my neck again, he wanted to say.

"Easy," Will said.

David opened his eye. His brother was behind Lucy now, frowning underneath his mask.

Lucy broke away. Will's face transformed when she turned to face him. He smiled for her. It looked pretty convincing, but David could tell he was pissed.

"I'm so glad you're alive," Lucy said. David grinned. It relieved him that she knew intuitively to be gentle with Will's ego.

"I missed you," Will said. He was brimming with energy, barely containing himself.

"Me too," Lucy said.

Will placed both his hands on her stomach.

"We're going to be okay now," Will said.

Startled, Lucy pushed his hand away.

"Don't—" Lucy said.

Will stumbled back, and Lucy's eyes went wide with regret. She took up both of Will's hands.

"I'm sorry," she said.

"It's—it's okay. I understand," Will said. "I know I've been a fuckup in the past and I've acted immature, but I've changed, Lucy. You've made me want to be someone better. I'm going to take care of you. And provide for you. Provide for our family. Lucy, I love you so much."

"Will, I . . ." She didn't continue. She looked to David.

"What?" Will said. "Why do you keep looking at him?"

"You need to know something," David said.

"This isn't about you, David," Will said, whipping a finger at David. He turned back to Lucy with open, yearning eyes. "What—what's going on?"

A Geek reached in and slapped David on the shoulder, hooted, and ran on. Will's eyes stayed locked on Lucy.

"The pregnancy didn't take," she said.

Will shook his head. "What are you talking about? Belinda said . . ."

"I lost it, Will. There was a baby, there was, and it was ours, and I tried to keep it safe but—" Lucy shuddered. "It's gone."

Will opened his mouth to speak, but stopped short. He didn't move. Like a VHS tape on pause—he was frozen, but still fidgeting. He stared at the ground. Through the ground. Lucy looked to David in a panic. He had no idea what to do either. He was afraid anything he said would set Will off. He wanted to tell him it would be all right. That this happens to couples a lot in the real world. That life goes on, and the important thing was that the three of them had survived. But he feared that Will would twist even those comforting words into malicious attempts to rub salt in his wounds.

"It's going to be okay," David said anyway. He couldn't not.

"WOOO HOO!" a Skater cried out as he raced past them.

Lucy went in for a hug, but not with all her heart like she'd hugged David. This was more tentative, like she feared Will was about to sprout thorns. He shook her off, and she backed away.

"You told him?" Will said, pointing at David. "He already knew?"

Lucy looked to David for the right answer.

"Will . . . yes, it was the first thing I asked her about. Just like you did. It's not some conspiracy—"

"No," Will said, sarcastic and vicious. "Of course not. Where would I get that idea? You two can barely keep your hands off each other. I guess this is the best thing that could'a happened, huh, Dave?"

"Will!" Lucy said.

"Choose," he said to Lucy. "You have to choose, right now. Is it him or me?"

Lucy gasped.

"Will, come on," David said.

"Shut up, David," Will said without looking at him. Will's eyes were locked on Lucy's. She couldn't look at him. Her eyes danced around, but she kept glancing at David.

"I should have known, right?" Will shouted. "Nothing ever changes."

"Will, don't say that," Lucy said.

"Then tell me I'm wrong. Tell me you love me and not David. And don't lie. Don't you dare lie to me now."

"I don't want to lie to you," Lucy said.

"So don't," Will said. His voice cracked as he said it, and his face flickered with anger right afterward, like he was mad at his throat for betraying him.

"We had our time, and it was good," Lucy said.

"Oh my God," Will said.

"It's not like those feelings weren't real—"

"Fuck you both," Will said.

"Will!" David cried.

Will stormed off. Lucy started crying. Will was cruising across the farm, straight for the front gate of the tractor-trailer wall.

"Stay here," David said.

David ran and caught up with Will, twenty feet from the exit. He tried to grab Will's arm, but Will threw him off.

"Come on, will you grow up?" David said.

Will stopped and faced him. "Go ahead. Take her. Take the glory, it's all for you, David."

"Nobody's out to get you, Will. Least of all me."

Will laughed, but it was short-lived, like a flower that wilted as it bloomed. His cheeks slackened, his eyes dulled. His stare became absent of feeling.

"I liked it better when you were dead," Will said.

Will walked to the exit, and David didn't stop him.

26

WILL HATED EVERYTHING. DAVID AND LUCY,
McKinley, the virus, the world.

The motorcycle he was riding was the only exception, because it was getting him out of Pale Ridge. He'd found it in the garage of an old couple who had lived down the street from him. It was exactly the kind of bike you'd expect an old person to ride—a bulky, maroon Honda Gold Wing with tons of storage compartments and room for two. To fill it, Will had siphoned gas out of a wrecked Subaru that had been wrapped around a tree. A motorcycle seemed perfect. It was the last thing David would want him to ride. His last motorcycle ride through the quad had made Lucy turn up her nose. Good. They could both go to hell. He cruised through the husk of Pale Ridge, and got used to how the hulking cycle turned. Before this, he'd only ridden a motorcycle in a straight line.

The more he saw of his dead town, the faster he wanted out

of it. He goosed the gas. Somewhere out there, far away, was a place where no one knew him, where no one knew that David was his brother; and where no one loved him, and where no one who could take their love away.

Now Leaving Pale Ridge, Colorado. Come back soon.

The sign zipped past, and Will pulled onto the two-lane interstate that extended ahead of him for miles. Heavy green forests crowded the road on both sides, and the asphalt was littered with leaves and twigs and debris like it hadn't been driven on for a while. Will poured on the gas and zoomed down the road.

Lucy had loved him once. He hadn't imagined it. Her love had felt so real to him. It had kept him going, kept him fighting, through everything he'd faced. Lucy's love had given him a reason to act right, it let him believe that he could be a man. But he didn't realize that her love had been provisional. She loved him, but only as long as David was dead.

Will accelerated. The trees whipped past.

He felt like a fool. He'd walked David right to her, not thinking that would tempt her. He'd assumed she'd want the same thing he did. God, it was laughable now. Dreaming about being the father of her child. He'd conjured the boy so clearly in his mind. He was like Will, but before he'd made any mistakes. Will was going to make sure the kid never messed up like he did. Those desires were the purest emotions he could remember experiencing. And he supposed they were real, and they were warranted, because at one point the baby had been alive. The sadness of it hollowed him. It ate at his insides.

Your baby is dead. Your baby is dead. Your baby is dead.

Will cranked the throttle, and felt the handlebars try to pull out of his hands. He hunkered down and gripped the bar harder, and clamped down on the rumbling beast with his thighs.

There had to be a way to blame it all on David, and he wanted to find it. The anger was there, but Will couldn't find the logic to support it. David had taken Lucy away, he tried to tell himself. But he hadn't. Lucy was the one who had turned her back on him. He knew he shouldn't have said what he had said to David. His brother had done nothing to harm him. But that was just the thing, David didn't *have* to do anything. Just as it had been for Will's whole life. All David had to do was walk into a room, and Will ceased to matter.

Will cranked the throttle, and the motor yelled. The forest was a blur of green in his periphery. The bike shook. Bugs pelted his face shield.

What a piece of shit Will was. A loser and a sore one. What had he accomplished by storming off? Did he really think it would change Lucy's mind to see him have a hissy fit? If anything, his behavior had probably done away with any doubt she might've had. All he'd done was cement her decision. He felt like a hurt little boy running away from home because he just got spanked. He wondered if—

Oh no.

Will felt a familiar sensation. A wrongness.

His brain became a vacuum, no thoughts, no words, no firm ground to stand on. He felt the bike fall away from him, even though it was still there. His eyes rolled back in his head, against his will. Then they jerked to the right, then left, and the last thing Will was aware of was the wobble of the motorcycle against his crotch, before the world disappeared.

He was tangled in a bush on the side of the road. There was pain in his head, all through his body. His brain spun. Dizzy and nauseous. His gas mask was intact. His faceless motorcycle helmet was still on over it. He looked down at his body and found everything still attached and bending in the correct directions. He'd gotten lucky.

David was right, Will shouldn't ride motorcycles. He shouldn't ride a bicycle. And he should have never skipped a day of taking his pills. Not enough food and water had undoubtedly made it worse. He'd been seizure-free for so long that he'd forgotten how easily his epilepsy could bitch-slap him, especially when he got himself worked up.

He was always trying to forget that he was epileptic, and prove that he didn't need anyone, but he did need someone. He'd always need someone.

Will kicked his leg free of the bush and planted it on the ground. Everything hurt. He wondered if he would ever learn. Would he always push people away when they tried to help? Would he always repel girls once they found out how much help he really needed, and realized that his tough act was just a desperate charade?

Will heard an approaching engine. He craned his neck to peer down the road, and he saw a giant white vehicle driving his way. It looked like a cross between a garbage truck and a double-decker bus. The windshield was black and he couldn't see through it, but the rest of the thing was painted glossy white. A giant red cross was painted on the front. The vehicle came to a stop thirty feet down the road from him, with a hiss from its air brakes.

A gentle female voice called out from the speaker on the roof.

"Are you infected?"

Will shook his aching head, and pointed to his gas mask.

A door opened on the side of the vehicle, and out walked three adults in white haz-mat suits. They approached Will, and when they got a few yards from him one of them raised a hand. It held a gray device that looked like a large garage door opener. With the click of a button the device fired a dart.

Will felt a sting in his leg, and looked down to see the dart protruding from his thigh. Its tail had a blinking blue diode.

"Virus-free," one of them said.

"Who are you?" Will said.

"We work for the government."

"You're military?" Will said. His stomach lurched.

"No," one of them said. "We're here to administer the cure."

LUCY WANTED TO SEE DAVID BY THE GOAL-

post. That was what Mort had told him, and David headed there right away. The parents and the infected were getting along just fine now. Some kids had left right away, to head for their families' houses, but many had stayed. The parents were tending to the kids like they'd been wishing they could do for two years, and the McKinley kids were soaking up the attention, regardless of whether it was from their own parents or not. Sam's dad seemed to have accepted the situation. He was showing some Freaks how to milk a cow, and do other things to help around the farm.

With the afternoon sun on his back, David walked behind the school to the football field. He looked for Lucy at the goalposts. One of them had been knocked down at some point, and the other goalpost was still standing, but he didn't see her by either. Then he heard a whistle.

There she was. Beyond the goalpost, Lucy stood on top of the farm wall. An extended aluminum construction ladder leaned against the top edge of the trailer wall, right by her feet. He didn't know why, but his heartbeat was beginning to hurry. He trotted over and stopped at the bottom of the ladder.

"What are you doing up there?" David said.

"Come up."

"What's up there?"

"Just come."

David did as she asked. When he stepped up onto the top of the trailer wall, Lucy pointed to the town side. He saw a station wagon parked just next to the wall, in the tall grass outside the farm. The back was stuffed with clothes, water, and supplies. She jingled a set of keys in her hand.

"Come with me," she said.

"Where?" he blurted, caught off guard.

"Anywhere else."

"I don't know," he said, but she ignored him and tugged on his arm.

"Let's leave. Just the two of us. This is all on the parents now. Let's get out of here. I trust you, David, I don't trust any-one else. We can be happy. I've got two full scuba tanks in that car. That oughta get us far enough until we can find some-thing else for you. We can take care of each other, and that can be enough. Just come. I know it's not the brave thing to do. But I have to get away from here. I never want to see this place again. Please, just come with me. Let's find some peace somewhere."

He wanted to. It sounded great to leave it all behind, but he felt guilt creeping up.

"Didn't I put them in this situation though?" he said.

"No. The virus did! Adults did. It's not your responsibility. Stop being such a good person for once, you dick. Let it be me and you. It can just be me and you. . . ."

She was in tears by the time she finished. He wiped her tears. She wanted to sit down, so they sat, and she wanted him to hold her, so he did. Before long they were lying on their backs, watching lazy clouds mosey across the sky. Time blurred. Reality became nothing but his arm around her, his hand clutched in hers, and the warmth that radiated from her body. He wasn't sure how long they lay there. He didn't know what to do, what to tell her, and he wasn't talking. Neither was she. It was as if neither of them wanted to speak for fear that the conversation could lead to them losing each other, and this feeling along with it. He wanted to get in the car with her and disappear. He did. But . . . Will.

"I just need to check for Will one more time. He might've come back," David said, breaking the extended silence.

"And then we'll go?"

David brushed her hair out of her face, but he didn't respond. He wanted to tell her yes, but his mouth wouldn't move.

"I'll wait for thirty minutes," Lucy said, "then I'm going."

The directness of her stare was serious. She would go. He believed her. It scared him, but it made him respect her more.

"See you soon," he said, and he touched the softness of her cheek.

"I hope so."

He hugged her. He tried to keep his demeanor light and positive, because Lucy wasn't smiling at all. He descended the ladder quickly, eager to be able to face the school and not see her sad eyes anymore.

David trudged back toward the school, knowing that if Will didn't return in the next thirty minutes, he would have a hard time choosing to leave. He might lose Lucy if he stayed. He might lose them both if he stayed. If he left with her, Will would never forgive him, but Will might not forgive him if he returned either. When had Will ever forgiven him for anything?

He heard the noise of all the students as he rounded the side of the school. They were cheering. David sped up to see what the celebration was about.

All of the McKinley kids were lined up in a tight formation, like they were about to do group calisthenics. There was a massive white vehicle unlike any he'd ever seen, with a red cross on it, and a group of adults in white haz-mat suits lined up in front of it, holding long white hoses that came off its roof. The hoses ended in spray guns. Standing beside the adults in the white haz-mat suits was Will in tattered clothes and wearing a gas mask. David was puzzled. Will stood on crutches, and he wore some sort of neck brace, but his shoulders were back, and he held his chin high. He was so far away that it was hard to tell, but he appeared to be smiling.

Pride puffed Will's chest. He looked over at the parents, practically bursting at the seams in anticipation. He saw mothers crying. He gazed at the faces of the kids waiting to be cured. A lot of them still munched the provisions the government people had handed out. He looked at Bobby's blacked-out head, and Bobby grinned back at him. None of the conflict between them mattered anymore. Will had made it all better. Will wondered what kind of life Bobby would have after this, with what he'd done to himself. But the same question applied to all of them. Bobby's change was skin-deep, but Will knew that everyone had been changed on the inside by their time in McKinley. How permanent were those changes? he wondered. Was everyone stronger because of them, or were they damaged goods? Could any of them ever get back to who they were before the school blew up?

Probably not.

Once his mother had passed away, Will had realized, you can never go back in life. You can only reminisce.

Still, the mood in the air was buoyant. He saw P-Nut hopping in place, unable to contain his excitement. He saw Zachary dancing gracefully with a smile on his face. He saw Ritchie, and Mort, and Colin, standing together in the back, instead of with their gangs, Loners once more. He hadn't spotted Lucy yet, but the crowd was tremendous. It was nearly everyone. He'd see her soon enough.

One of the hose holders signaled back to the truck, and Will heard a low buzz. Pressurized, white fog sprayed out from the hoses in great plumes, and the men holding the spray guns angled them so that the fog shot over the heads of the entire crowd, then slowly settled onto them.

Will continued to search for Lucy in the crowd as McKinley kids danced in the descending fog, and held their hands up toward the sky. *Where was she?* He wanted her to know he wasn't all bad. He wanted to see her joy as he took all of her problems away.

Something caught his eye in the distance. David stood by the side of the school. He raised his hand in the air, like he was reaching out to Will over all that distance, and Will raised his back. He wished he could communicate everything he felt through the way he raised his hand. He wanted his brother to know that he was sorry. That he didn't mean it. He loved him and he always would, no matter what kind of fight they got into.

Thump.

Will turned backed to the crowd to see P-Nut lying on his stomach, a thick froth of black blood gushing from his mouth.

Thump-thump-th-thump. Kids went limp and crumpled to the ground like rag dolls, spraying black blood and glops of tissue from their mouths as they fell. Black blood arced through the air. Mouths became geysers. Bodies piled onto bodies. Other students fled. He saw them shoot a kid with the same blinking blue dart they'd hit Will with, then the diode turned red and the kid coughed black sludge and dropped.

"Stop!" Will cried. "What are you doing?"

The campus was chaos. Infected fled past David, away from the white fog, where thick streams of black blood flung through the air like a casino water-fountain show. David dashed toward Will. His brother was trying to tear one of the hoses away from a man in a haz-mat suit. David couldn't process what was happening. He saw parents trying to help the kids escape. He saw Bobby's mother shoving him into a pickup truck. He saw other parents fighting the men in the white haz-mat suits, trying to stop the massacre.

He was still so far from Will. He watched his brother lunge at the man holding the hose, and tear at the material of his haz-mat suit, trying to rip it open. He could see the panic in the way the man jerked back and strained to get away from Will. One of the guy's buddies rushed up to help, and he had a rifle.

The man leveled the rifle at Will.

A spray of red burst from Will's head, and David heard the

shot a moment later. The tiny shape of Will's skull looked wrong for a second, like an apple with a bite taken out of it, then Will dropped like a bag of rocks.

The shock wiped David's mind blank. He wasn't aware of turning around and running. He just knew his feet were pumping and he couldn't catch his breath, and he was halfway to the wall, and Will was dead. So many were dead. The aluminum ladder glinted in the sunlight up ahead. Fleeing infected were climbing it and jumping the wall. David reached the ladder and climbed. When he got to the top, infected were running for the woods. He looked for Lucy below him, and he saw tire tracks that tore a path through the tall grass, all the way to the road.

28

IT WAS GOING TO BE A BEAUTIFUL DAY. DAVID
could feel the first crispness of fall in the morning air. It was
a primal thing, the way a change in the weather could alter a
person's mood. The whisper of leaves, the sparkle of the sun,
the trees turning the color of pumpkins and roses made him
happy. He welcomed that feeling.

The gravel in the driveway crackled under his boots. He
opened the back of the Jeep and tossed in his bag. The car was
the exact same year and model as the one he used to have,
the one he used to drive Will to school. His father had bought
it for him, in an effort to restore a sense of normalcy, but
it just made him think of Will. In the Jeep, when the music
was loud enough, and the wind whipped hard enough to
strip everything away, David could feel Will sitting beside
him, in the passenger seat, laughing at how hard he was
rocking out.

David clicked the back door shut, trying not to make too much noise.

"David," his dad said.

Too late.

David turned around. His father stood on the porch, still in his plaid pajamas. A beige mug of coffee steamed in his hand and he blocked out the morning sun by holding a folded magazine up to his brow. He still had a little bit of bed head. David loved his dad, and felt so lucky that he'd been able to track him all the way to Nebraska, but he hated seeing the guy in his pjs. He couldn't explain it.

He'd found his dad in a town at the border of the infected zone, where the military had been releasing McKinley graduates earlier in the quarantine. His dad had spent a year and a half watching other parents get reunited with their children, until the day the government had told the parents that there had been a gas leak in McKinley, and that all of their children were dead. When David had shown up on his father's doorstep, his dad had fallen to his knees. He'd thought he'd lost his son forever.

"Where are you going?"

"I, uh, I've got to take another trip."

His dad stepped down from the porch. David's instinct was to get in the Jeep, but that would come off as rude. And he didn't want to make his dad feel insecure. He knew how guilty his dad already felt for not being among the parents who'd helped the school, or that he hadn't somehow, some way stopped that bullet from entering Will's brain. David didn't want to make his dad feel worse by thinking his only remaining son hated him.

"You just got back from your last trip, David. Why don't you stay? I've still got a month of leave at work. We haven't had one solid week yet to just . . . hang out."

His dad tucked the magazine under his arm and rubbed the back of David's head. He glanced at David's eye patch, then looked to the ground, and looked back to David's good eye. He did that occasionally, as if the sight of the injury overloaded his brain, and he had to descramble it.

"I'm sorry about that. I really am, but there's a lot that goes into getting a farm on its feet."

"But you're not even at the farm."

"I'm piecing together the workforce."

"There's plenty of people around that are out of work, David. All you've gotta do is put a job post online."

David wasn't sure, but it felt like this was the thousandth time they'd had this conversation.

"Dad—"

"I know, I know. That's not the point. But you've got enough trouble as it is being registered as a former infected. I just . . . I just worry that you're only making things harder for yourself by going state to state and consorting with more of them."

"These people I'm 'consorting' with—they're my friends. And a lot of them don't have any place to go, *because* they've been registered and no one wants anything to do with them."

"I understand that. I've seen kids like that around, begging for change, but you're not like that, David. You're a good kid. And you've got me. I mean, why can't these other kids go be with their families?"

"I am their family," David said.

His dad tried to answer, but couldn't. So, he took a sip of coffee. He looked down the wooded driveway to the road at the bottom of the hill, then to the Jeep.

"How you doing on gas?"

"I've got a half tank."

"Well, there's not a working station until you get to—"

"I know. I'll make it."

"Do you have cash, because cards don't work like they used to—"

"I know. I've got some."

"You know. You know," his dad said with a touch of frustration. "Well, I guess I better shut up, then."

David gave his father a hug. His father held him tight.

"You're doing a good thing, David. You're a good kid. It's just hard for me. I want to keep you safe."

David nodded and patted his father's back. He knew his dad was crying even though he couldn't see his face over his shoulder. His voice was plump.

"I wish your mom could see the man you are now," he said. "She'd take one look at you and shove an elbow in my ribs and say 'Told you so.'"

David laughed, and his father let him go.

"I'll call you when I get there," David said.

"Where's there?"

"Canada."

David's dad shook his head with an exasperated grin.

"Get outta here," he said.

David gave his dad a wave and got in the Jeep. He started it up. The purr of the engine excited him. He had a long trip ahead, but that was always his favorite part. To watch the world go by, to know that there were thousands of miles of road ahead of him. Sam's dad had started a new farm in rural Nebraska on the same model as the one in Pale Ridge, only this one employed the previously infected rather than keeping them locked up. David was trying to find former McKinley kids to work there. So many ex-infected had scattered to the wind after graduating. And David was making himself an expert on finding them, especially former Loners. He'd found Nelson in Reno spinning signs for a used car lot and doing a bad job of it. He'd found the twins living in an abandoned amusement park in Texas, living off berries and mushrooms. Belinda had been the easiest to find. She was working as a waitress at a truck stop in Hays, Kansas, and generally hating life. He'd found Loners living in storm drains and abandoned houses. That had become the norm for much of Colorado's teen population who hadn't been welcomed back by their families, or who had ventured out into the world only to find their loved ones dead. And so they traveled, looking for someplace to call home, where they weren't persecuted or driven off by locals who wanted to keep their communities "clean."

He'd heard about others. Zachary had written David a letter and said that he'd phased out of infection and was living in New York. He was doing costumes for a small theatre company there, dating up a storm, and he'd changed his name to Dane. David had heard from Gonzalo that Kemper, the old leader of the Nerds, was working in the back of an electronics store in Santa Fe. He said Kemper was consumed with the goal of getting into MIT, and that he'd cried when Gonzalo told him that Violent had died. Each of the two times David had crossed paths with Gonzalo he'd tried to give him any info he could to help in the big guy's ongoing search for Sasha. Gonzalo's hope was uncrushable.

David turned up the stereo. The wind howled. He'd found thirteen McKinley kids in just about two months. It felt good to be busy. It helped to fill the void in his heart.

A vision of Will being shot in the head seized David.

He jolted and slammed on the brakes. He gripped the steering wheel and squeezed with all the power in his fists until his breathing slowed.

He had a new lead to follow, and he prayed that it was real.

He threw the Jeep into first gear and started driving again. He'd seen a lot of familiar faces recently, and had helped them find a better life, but if this lead panned out, he'd get to see the one face he missed most of all.

29

LUCY WAS GETTING FAT. SHE BLAMED HER
mother and her grandmother. They were the ones who had
stocked Lucy's kitchen full of rich food from the local gour-
met markets. They said they couldn't help themselves. They
were so happy to have her back. Every morning, she'd find a
care package waiting for her. She stood in front of her open
cabinets, staring at all of her options. She'd been "quarantined" in her grandparents' guesthouse for a little over two
months, and still she couldn't help but marvel at the bounty
in her cupboard.

There was sweet peach chutney, strawberry black pepper-
corn fruit spread, French lemon curd, apricot salsa dulce, and
cinnamon-infused maple syrup. There was faux foie gras,
homemade olive bread, wild boar terrine, and lobster pâté.
She could choose between Tasmanian leatherwood honey and
raw thistle honey, whatever those were. Pumpkin butter, fig

and olive relish, white truffle mayonnaise, fire-roasted poblano peppers, champagne garlic mustard, cherry tomatoes in oil, and summer sausages—that was just one small shelf. She'd experimented with crazy combinations. Her favorite was pickles dipped in Sir Kensington's Spiced Scooping Ketchup. It did taste great, but mostly she just liked saying it. She'd consumed so much sugar she was sure she'd start sweating frosting soon. Saltwater taffy, hot cashew brittle, marzipan fruit, key lime chocolate wafers, dark chocolate caramel apples. She liked to start her day with handmade vanilla marshmallows and coffee sweetened with rock candy swizzle sticks. For lunch she'd have stomachaches. And then, there was Lucy's fridge. She had cheeses from nearly every country in the UN. Sharp, extra sharp, soft, semisoft, spreadable. She was surrounded by so much food these days that she was starting to forget what it felt like to be hungry. Not that she minded.

The weeks following the massacre at McKinley had drawn on every survival skill Lucy had learned in McKinley. She'd fled into a landscape where the government's last push to eradicate the virus had been in high gear. Tremendous quantities of "the cure" had been manufactured and distributed to police and citizens all across the United States. Infected were getting cured left and right, if they didn't get a bullet in the head first. Lucy had driven north from Pale Ridge until she'd run out of gas. She'd had no money, no food, and she was the enemy. For a moment, she'd considered trying to steal fuel, but any human interaction meant the chance of death—if not for her, then for them. And killing Gates had been enough murder for this lifetime. At two a.m., with a handful of change, at the only pay phone in Rapid City, South Dakota, Lucy had faced down one of her greatest fears: finding out if her parents were alive or dead. She'd dialed her father's cell phone number, praying that it wasn't disconnected.

The call had gone through and she'd heard her father's voice for the first time in two years.

Within twenty-four hours, Lucy had found herself hidden in a cargo truck, crossing the border into Canada. She was sealed inside a crate that was meant to contain artisanal patio bricks, but really had half a futon on the floor, a battery-powered reading lamp, a stack of magazines, a box of meal replacement bars, water, and a bedpan. Not the most fragrant of environments after the first twelve hours. After she was through with the magazines, and after she had lain or sat in every position possible in her four-by-four-foot box, she had been dying to stand, and on the cusp of losing her mind. The box had been jostled and battered around, and there had always been rumbling. Lucy had never known where she was.

When the top had finally popped off and she had seen her parents and grandparents in haz-mat suits, looking down at her with tears in their eyes, she had felt like she was being born anew. Lucy remembered looking around at her grandparents' lush estate and seeing the world as titanic. Endless. She'd thought the feeling would've passed in the days after, but it hadn't. They'd set her up in the guesthouse, where they'd sealed all the windows and vents shut. They talked to her every day on the phone, standing just outside her window. Even now, weeks later, she still found the world breathtaking in its enormity, and Lucy was grateful to be a tiny part of it all, to be part of her family, to be one of the living.

South of the border, the US government touted victory. The claim was that there were no more infected. It was all over the news, with a public divided over the morality of how the job had been done. Canadian news coverage was more condemnatory, mainly because the virus hadn't made it to Canada. The reports were always hard for Lucy to watch. They made her think of what had happened at McKinley, and how the kids had come spilling over the top of the farm wall, climbing the fence, running for their lives, and how she'd gunned it out of there. How she had left David behind. How she'd seen Ritchie while she was on the run, and he'd told her that Will had been killed.

All the food in the world, this safe house she lived in, and all the love her family could pile on her, none of it could heal the crack that ran through her heart now that Will was gone. She appreciated her family more than she could put into words, but her sorrow couldn't be pacified. None of her good fortune made it all right that Will's life had stopped that day.

There was a knock at the kitchen door.

The door had a window panel in it, and there was David on the other side. She nearly fainted. He mimed the action of opening the door. He smiled behind the face shield of his mask. Lucy unlocked the door. This was crazy. No one in her family liked to come inside, none of them had. They were too afraid, but here came David in a gas mask, walking in like it was nothing. She swore the colors in the room grew richer and more luminous as soon as he'd entered. He still had that power over her, a gravitational pull that she couldn't fight.

"I can't believe you're here."

He hugged her right away, and it felt good to be touched again.

"You're alive," David said. He squeezed harder. "Thank God, you're alive."

"You too," she said. It was the best response she could summon, her emotions were swarming on her.

They separated enough to look into each other's eyes. She wanted to kiss him.

"I'm still infected," she said.

"Yeah, your parents told me."

"I really wanna make out."

David laughed. He pinched her arm playfully as they separated, and then he bopped around the kitchen, checking the place out.

"So, how many bathrooms you got here? Is there more than one bedroom?"

"What are you, apartment hunting?"

"I was thinking about it."

"What do you mean?"

David's jovial manner grew more serious.

"I want to be around. To make sure you transition out and everything turns out fine. I already talked to your folks about it."

"You mean stay here? In this house, in a gas mask all day and night?"

David shrugged. "Yeah."

"It could be months."

"I left you behind once, and you had to face McKinley alone. I can't forgive myself for that."

"You're too hard on yourself," she said.

He shook his head.

"I'm not going anywhere until I know you're okay."

"Now I'm really upset that we can't kiss," she said with a little laugh and a few tears.

He walked to her and took her hands in his.

"Will you give me a tour?" he said.

Lucy's smile went away. She knew David hadn't meant

to say his brother's name, but hearing David say the word *will* made her blood go cold.

"I'm so sorry about Will," she said.

David's light and airy demeanor crumbled.

"He . . . ," David said, but couldn't find the words. She saw a deep anguish in him that matched her own and far exceeded it. If she had a crack in her heart, David must have a chasm.

Lucy's cell phone rang. It was her mom's phone technically, but she'd been using it. Her mom was calling. It was pretty much always her mom calling. She walked into the living room, to the window that faced the main house, and saw her mother rushing up the sloped lawn. Her mom's baggy linen outfit was fluttering in the wind, and she shook her phone in her outstretched hand. She was in such a hurry that she'd left the door hanging open in the big house behind her. Her mom never did that. Lucy answered the call as her mother ran.

"Mom, what's wrong?"

"Lucy, I don't know how to tell you this," her mom said as she made it to the window and put her fingers to the glass. There was a glob of blackberry jelly on her mom's blouse.

"What? You're scaring me," Lucy said.

"It's just—" Her mom's mascara was smeared. She'd been crying. "I'm going to patch your uncle in."

Uncle Phillip? Her uncle was a physician, and he'd come to give her a checkup a week ago to make sure her injuries were healing properly. They'd sworn that he was family and she could trust him, but now she wondered if that was true.

There was a quiet click.

"Hello, Phillip, are you there?" her mom said.

"Yes, you got me," Phillip said.

"Okay, Lucy's on too. Can you tell her what you told me?"

There was a pause.

"You haven't said anything?" Phillip said.

"I—couldn't," her mom said.

Phillip took a deep breath. It sounded like radio static when he blew it out.

"Well, all right. Hey, Lucy," he said.

"Uh . . . hey, Uncle Phillip."

"I'll get to the point, kiddo. I ran your blood work," Phillip continued, "and, honey, uh . . . you're pregnant."

Lucy nearly dropped the phone.

"What do you mean, I'm pregnant?"

"What?" David said, and walked over to her.

His eyes were full of hope.

"I . . . ," Lucy said.

"There's nothing to be ashamed of," her mother said.

David grabbed her phone and pressed speakerphone.

"That's not possible," Lucy said at her phone with a hint of anger. "I told you—in confidence, Uncle Phillip"—she glanced at her mother through the window and cringed—"that I had a miscarriage."

"I know you did," her uncle said.

Lucy turned away from the window. She didn't want to see what her mom was feeling.

"Well, I wasn't lying about it, believe me," she said.

"I don't think you were," Uncle Phillip said.

"Then what are you . . ."

"You were pregnant with twins."

Joy and heartache swirled within Lucy. David hugged her and didn't let go.

"I can't believe it. I'm gonna be an uncle." David said with wonder.

Since the first day of school, she'd always been afraid of what was around the corner, but now Lucy could see a future with David stretching out before her and the fear wasn't there. Still, her mind reeled.

"Uncle Phillip, it doesn't make sense to me," Lucy said.

"It's not that uncommon. A lot of pregnancies start out as twins," her uncle said. "To put it simply, early in your pregnancy there were two fetuses, and at some point—"

He coughed, and cleared his throat.

"The weaker one died."

ACKNOWLEDGMENTS

When we began working on *Quarantine*, writing even a single novel seemed like an impossible challenge. Now, four years later, we are authors of an insane trilogy that we love, and we've been happy to discover that other people love it too. We're grateful to everyone who has ever read a *Quarantine* book and told a friend about it.

We'd also like to thank:

Andrea Cascardi, Erin Molta, Margaret Coffee, Michelle Bayuk, and our team at Egmont for giving us the freedom to make bold choices every step of the way.

Mollie Glick and everyone at Foundry for seeing the potential in *Quarantine* from the start.

Greg Ferguson for his guidance in crafting the ultimate high school nightmare.

Elizabeth Law for taking a chance on us.

Rachel Miller and Jesse Hara for their encouragement and support.

Kami Garcia for her unflappable enthusiasm for *Quarantine*.

Daniel Kraus for always seeing our story for what it was and being the first to tell the world about it.

And so many others who helped us along the way, in big ways and small, like Peter Beck, Jen Bigheart, Duncan Birmingham, Aaron Buckwalter, Cy and Genevieve Carter, Mary Elizabeth Day, LeVette Fuller, Erin Gross, Franklin Hardy, Karen Jensen, Ian Kemmer, Elisa Kemmer, John Kneedler, Lane Kneedler, Susan Kneedler, Tara Kole, Shane Kosakowski, Heather McCallum, Chris and Frances Merrill, Curtis Nishimura, Michelle Pak, Lauren Peugh, Mary Rolich, Will Richter, AJ Rinella, Susan Robertson, Katie Robbins, Geoffrey Rose, Loretto Seles, Andrew Seles, Kirsten Smith, Louis Tocchet, Clay Tweel, Andrea Vuleta, Jeffrey West, Stephanie Wilkes, Richard Wilkinson, and the YA Sisterhood.

Lex, in particular, would like to thank:

Every friend who bought a book or rallied for a book signing; Eluria, his grandmother, who couldn't get enough *Quarantine*, even if she thought there was too much cussing; his parents, who never hesitated to say, "Go for it."; Geoffrey and Noelle, Geoffrey and Kate, and Peter, who endured a working stiff on sunny summer days with humor and understanding; Matt and Staci for being such thoughtful and generous friends during the final push of this series; and finally Alexis for her patience, love, and confidence, and for being an advisor like no other.

Thomas, in particular, would like to thank his parents, who have been his greatest supporters; his favorite painting teachers, Thomas Sgouros and Trent Burelson, for their art lessons that continue to shape his craft; his sixth grade English teacher, Mr. Rosenwald, who told him that the point of life was to have fun; his high school English teacher Mrs. Solari for enduring his antics; Angela Trimbur for her love and inspiration; and his entire family—his aunts and uncles, brother and cousins—for being his biggest fans.

Without the help we received from all of you, *Quarantine* may never have happened.

TURN THE PAGE TO READ
THE FIRST TWO CHAPTERS OF

THE GIANT

A NEW BOOK SET IN THE WORLD
OF *THE QUARANTINE SERIES*,
ABOUT GONZALO'S JOURNEY ACROSS
A RAVAGED AMERICA
TO FIND HIS BELOVED SASHA.

AVAILABLE IN HARDCOVER AND EBOOK
JULY 2016

1

GONZALO STARED INTO THE EYES OF THE mountain lion. It had emerged from the woods, under the purple light of dusk, slunk into the middle of the road and stopped. Now the animal gazed at him unblinking, and completely still. Not even a twitch of a whisker. This was bad. Gonzalo had no weapon, and no car to drive away.

The lion seemed to be thinking. Sizing him up. Deciding whether to pounce.

Gonzalo was big, and that tended to keep him out of fights. If things ever got as far as Gonzalo making a fist, the other guy would see that Gonzalo's fist was the size of a car battery and lose his nerve.

Gonzalo made his hands into fists. The mountain lion took a step toward him.

This wasn't a person, this was an animal. It killed on instinct. It was born knowing how to rip the flesh out of another animal's neck with its mouth. It had no more inner conflict over the morality of the act than Gonzalo did grocery shopping.

The lion lowered its head below its shoulders. Its round green eyes were buried inside a heavy brow and massive cheekbones. Little black pupils like bullet holes stayed aimed at Gonzalo's eyes, never straying.

No human could outrun a mountain lion, especially not him. Running was something that Gonzalo could do for about five minutes before the effort of propelling all two hundred and ninety pounds of him forward would have him gagging for air.

Gonzalo glanced behind him. There was a bicycle within reach in the tall grass, next to a human skeleton wearing a bicycle helmet. A neon spandex shirt was loose over the rib-cage and black spandex shorts sagged between the hip bones.

The mountain lion growled from deep in its belly. Gonzalo looked back at those deadly black pupils as he edged toward the bicycle. The lion watched.

Gonzalo bent down slowly with his eyes on the animal, and grasped hold of the bicycle's curved handlebar. The mountain lion took three steps toward him. Its legs moved gracefully, its muscles bulging like rocks under its fur. Its head stayed low. Gonzalo pulled the bicycle up off the ground and the long grass that was tangled in its spokes and gears tore with a dry, raspy rip. It was painfully loud. velcro wallet in a movie theatre. Each pop of a grass blade snapping seemed enough to provoke an attack. The animal's advance was unhurried. Its front paws stretched far out in front with each step, ready to spring forward at any moment.

Gonzalo went for the bike. He ripped it up, threw his leg over, got his butt on the tiny seat and pounced on the pedals. He was wobbling on the pitted asphalt a second later, and he could feel on his skin that sharp claws were about to dig canals down his back, and mighty fangs were going to clamp down on his neck. He pumped his feet in a frenzy, weaving down the road, willing himself to go faster and faster, the forest on either side whipping past in his peripheral vision, until his legs were about to quit.

The bite never came. When Gonzalo finally looked back, the mountain lion wasn't chasing him. It wasn't watching him either. It wasn't there at all. The beast had lost interest and wandered off. Gonzalo allowed his pace to slow. The bike seat was the size of a child's sneaker. It felt like a medieval torture device trying to split him in half. Gonzalo spat out a slew of curses. He couldn't believe he was in this situation. Just two days before, he'd had wheels, weapons, a gas mask — he'd had an entire van full of supplies. His search for Sasha had already gone on for six months, and it'd taken him exactly that long to assemble all that gear. He'd had one ax, and three sledgehammers. Weeks of food that he'd stockpiled, fishing gear, galoshes, hiking boots. It had taken him months to find boots that fit his enormous feet. The same was true of the van. It was one of the only cars he'd been able to find that he could fit inside. And someone had gone and stolen it when he was bathing in a creek. The notes he'd been keeping on his search for Sasha, six months of clues, gone. The phone he'd had since before the quarantine, the one that contained every picture he had ever taken of Sasha, lost forever. If he failed in his mission to find her out here in the infected zone, he would never see her face again.

Gonzalo slowed to a coast and pulled a pack of cigarettes and a lighter out of his pocket. At least he still had his smokes. He fished one out with his lips and lit it, his hands still shaking from the rush of the lion encounter. He'd picked up a little habit since graduation. Hadn't really intended to, but there wasn't much in the infected zone that made you feel good anymore. Cigarettes, though, you could still find around. His mom would have killed him if she knew. He took a deep drag and relaxed a little. He never felt safe in the infected zone, but his smokes helped take the edge off. He was going to quit as soon as he found Sasha and got back to the real world. Gonzalo put the pack and lighter in his pocket and pedaled back up to a respectable speed.

The sun had sunk below the horizon, and it would be dark soon. The purple sky had darkened to a deep violet. The road up ahead was getting harder to see. He needed new wheels, preferably a vehicle like the van, big enough for him to sleep inside. If he couldn't find something soon, abandoned by the side of the road, he'd need to find some other kind of shelter. He needed a weapon. He didn't care what it was, but he'd go for the most frightening one he could find. His favorite kind of fight was the one that never started, the kind that was about to start until you pulled out a chainsaw splattered with red paint and the guy thought better of it and ran. He needed water and food. He needed more clothes than the shorts and t-shirt he was wearing. Thank God he had his high tops. If he was barefoot, he'd probably step on a rusty nail, get gangrene and—

Something caught his eye in the dark woods to the left. A pair of luminescent green eyes in the darkness, staring at him and matching his pace.

Before he could react, the mountain lion burst from the forest, cut across the road and launched itself into the air. The lion swatted him off the bike with a heavy paw. Gonzalo's back hit the asphalt, and instantly the monster was on him, open jaws, rows of sharp teeth bared. It lowered its head to chomp down on the soft flesh of his throat, but Gonzalo threw his arm up. The lion's fangs sank into the meat of his forearm instead. He tried to yank his arm away, but the lion's jaws only clamped down harder. The strength of its bite was terrifying. Like a pickup truck parked on his forearm. Its brow was twisted in a knot, its snout bunched into rolls of bristling fur. Its eyeballs glistened in the fading light, spherical and green and furious.

It opened its jaws wide and its fangs withdrew from his flesh. It went for his neck again. Gonzalo sacrificed his arm again, except this time its fangs buried into his bicep. He didn't have long. The beast was stronger, it would be digging into his neck in no time.

Gonzalo shoved his fingers so deep into the lion's right eye socket that he could feel the rope of optic nerve between his fingers. He gripped the eyeball. It felt like an oiled plum. The lion yowled, unclamped its jaws and whipped its head away from Gonzalo. The eye, however, stayed with Gonzalo. The maimed lion thrashed around, violently shaking its head, then bounded off into the woods.

Gonzalo panted in the steadily growing darkness. The lion's eyeball slid off his palm. He lifted himself up and stumbled sideways. He had a lot of holes in his arm. Blood poured down to his fingertips and dripped down to the road. He made sure that this muscles still worked and all of his fingers could flex and extend, but the effort made the pain swell. He'd have to find a way to treat his wounds soon, or they might get infected.

He plucked the pack of cigarettes from his pocket, shook one out, and lit up. Maybe the nicotine buzz would make his arms hurt less, he thought. Cool wind shook the trees like pom poms as the smoke kissed his lungs.

Gonzalo leaned over and picked up his bike. It didn't seem to be too damaged. After a few more puffs, he got back on the bike and peddled to a shaky start. Stupid tiny bike. He probably looked like a circus bear riding this thing. The bicycle wobbled underneath him at this low speed, and he had to crank the handlebars back and forth to keep from tipping over. He pedaled faster, his knees nearly striking his chest, and the bike picked up enough speed to steady him. The rear wheel squeaked with every rotation.

He thought of Sasha.

THE QUAD WAS AN OCEAN OF VIOLENCE. HAIR
colors smashed into each other. The pile of packaged food
and supplies in the center of the quad would be completely
gone soon. Gonzalo clutched a can of corn in his hand like
it was a gold brick. He'd scooped the can up when another
kid had dropped it. A can of corn was way more than Gonzalo
thought he'd get today. Now, it was just a matter of getting off
the battlefield alive.

Gonzalo ran as fast as his runty legs could carry him.
Everything about him was tiny compared to the other kids.
The other boys his age didn't just have bigger bodies, they
had deeper voices too. Gonzalo was still the hairless boy he'd
been when he'd started junior high, and he was beginning to
think that puberty would never strike. He was sixteen, but he
looked twelve. The Freak mob in front of him towered over
him by at least a foot. As they slowed down, he slowed down.

He dodged a Nerd who lunged for his can, and kept running. Gonzalo glanced back to see if the Nerd was still chasing him and saw the kid get flattened by the entire Varsity defensive line, which was charging right for Gonzalo.

He tried to run faster. Those yellow-haired monsters were set to bulldoze him in seconds. Gonzalo cut right in the hope that he could get out of their path. Ahead of him, a trio of Geeks were dragging a palette of gallon-sized water jugs back to the sidelines. When they saw the Varsity wall of death behind Gonzalo, they abandoned the pallet and fled. Gonzalo tried to turn and avoid the water jugs, but someone tackled him from behind. His face hit the plastic jugs, and another heavy Varsity guy landed on top of him, crushing his chest into the wooden palette.

Varsity hollered as they dove on top of each other to pile onto Gonzalo. The weight of this mound of muscle and bone squeezed all the air out of his lungs. Gonzalo began to panic. He was going to suffocate. He felt the wood splintering underneath him. His ribcage was going to cave in. His skull was about to pop. Muffled voices yelled and cheered and laughed above him.

When the Varsity pile finally climbed off him and started collecting the water jugs, one of them picked Gonzalo up by the arm pits and threw him to another Varsity, who threw him to another. The Varsity guys played catch with him like he was a ball. They thought it was hilarious. Gonzalo didn't. He still clutched the can of soup. Despite everything, he'd held onto it. The next guy trying to catch him fumbled the catch, and Gonzalo was able to scurry away.

He wove through a crowd of Geeks and Freaks that were fighting. He dove between people's legs, he hunched over as he ran, all to make Varsity lose track of him. Ahead, Gonzalo saw a guy twice his size get two teeth knocked out in a fight over powdered pancakes. He saw a Nerd girl get dragged to the ground by three Skater girls who wanted her pants.

He dashed in the direction of the nearest hallway, desperate to get away from the whirling elbows, the gnashing teeth, the packs of kids who hunted together like wolves, but something caught his eye. A tiny Slut, with her red hair in a high pony tail. She was smaller than him, which was rare, and she was carrying a bag of rice away from the Slut food pile, toward the hall. She turned and looked right at him, and she was smoking hot. His pace slowed to a jog. For a moment, he forgot where he was. She had definitely stared right at him, from across the quad. And nobody stared at him. Nobody even glanced at him, especially not a pretty girl. He watched her disappear into the hall.

Gonzalo snapped out of his trance and broke into a sprint. The open doors of the hallway were twenty feet ahead. Once he got there, he could hide. He could eat. He was going to enjoy prying open that can and filling his stomach full of corn in some dark, hidden corner of the school. Two tall guys were fighting up ahead, to his left, and just as Gonzalo tried to zip past them, one guy's wild punch clocked Gonzalo in the side of the jaw.

When Gonzalo opened his eyes again, he was on his stomach in the dirt, and people were stomping on him. No, not stomping on him, people were running over him, stepping on his back like he was the ground. He blinked to clear his vision and pushed himself up to his hands and knees. His can of corn was gone. The two guys who'd been fighting, gone too. A flood of Sluts ran past. He didn't know how long he'd been out, but the food drop was still going strong.

Gonzalo crawled to the hallway, coughing and sputtering, with a sore jaw, a thumping head, blurred vision and no food. When he finally hit the linoleum floor of the hallway, he wanted to kiss it.

He couldn't keep running in the drops like this. He knew he'd starve if he tried to keep going it alone. If he had other people looking out for him, he'd be okay. He needed to join a gang. Any gang. It was the only way he'd be able to survive. There was only one problem.

He didn't like people.

Gonzalo had never been a big talker, he'd always been the quiet kid; but it had been three months since McKinley had been quarantined, and Gonzalo hadn't spoken to anyone.

In the early days that had been alright. People had assumed he was just a little more shell-shocked than everyone else, and they'd given him food and tried to help him. As time had gone on though, their pity for him had waned, and he'd become the weird, silent kid that the others avoided. Eventually, people had stopped helping each other altogether. No one wanted to share their food anymore, especially not with him.

He was terrified every day now. Terrified of running in the drops, of starving, of the bigger kids in the halls, which was pretty much everyone. He was terrified of this virus they all had. He was terrified about the fact that they had no idea what was happening outside. But as scared as he was of all these things, Gonzalo never let it show. That was his one strength — he could remain stoic in the face of anything. He had always been like that. His father was like that, and so was his grandfather. They were giant, barrel-chested men. Biggest guys in the neighborhood, they were real proud of that. Gonzalo was too. His father's face seemed chiseled out of stone. His grandfather's was the same, except his was a giant stone on a rocky shore that had been eroded over time and covered in salt deposits and barnacles. Neither of their faces ever moved. And they barely ever spoke. Even if Gonzalo wasn't big like them, he could be tough like them. He could keep his face still, his mouth in a frown and his eyes mean no matter what was happening around him. Thinking about this now, all he wanted was to be back home on the living room couch , watching TV with his father and grandfather in their separate easy chairs, and not saying a word, while his mom and sister zipped around the house like whirling tops, chatting endlessly with each other, or on the phone, or at them.

Gonzalo made his way to the administrative offices, where the Skaters lived. When he got there, a group of them were prying the linoleum tiles off the floor of the hallway, while the rest of them seemed to be goofing off. He'd join any gang that would have him at this point, but the Skaters looked like they knew how to have a good time. They were always laughing about something, or messing around on their skateboards, having fun despite this terrible situation everybody was in. Their leader, a kid who called himself P-Nut, launched through the air on a skateboard and landed it on a wooden desk in the middle of the hall. He tried to kick-flip off it, but totally biffed the landing and fell laughing into a gaggle of Skater girls. They looked eager to catch him. When P-Nut threw one leg forward, grabbed a doe-thin girl in a belly shirt, dipped her like Zorro and kissed her, Gonzalo wanted to be him.

Gonzalo approached one of the Skaters. The guy's head was shaved except for a round patch of hair on each side of his head, which he'd tinted gray and gelled into bull horns. He wanted to ask bull horns if he could join. He looked him in the eye and tried to say the words, but his face didn't move.

"Can I help you with something?" the Skater said, looking down at him.

Gonzalo tried. He couldn't even get his lips to part.

"Why are you looking at me like that, shrimp?" The Skater said.

It was like the connection between Gonzalo's brain and the muscles of his face had been cut. He tried to force himself to get the words out.

"Check out how this kid's fuckin' lookin' at me. I asked you what you want, kid."

It's probably better this way, he thought. They'll hear the fear in your voice if you talk. They'll know they can mess with you.

Gonzalo's mouth remained in a frown, his eyes stayed mean and unflinching. Other Skaters gathered at the doorway, behind the bull-horned kid. Gonzalo didn't know what to do. The seconds ticked away.

"I think you better get the fuck out of here, shrimp. How 'bout that?" the Skater said.

Gonzalo didn't like this guy. He was mad at Gonzalo for nothing. Gonzalo didn't like his friends either. All of their hairstyles were stupid. Still, for the sake of food and protection, and a chance to be around girls, Gonzalo tried to put his feelings aside. He just had to open his mouth and ask one question — can I be in your gang? All that happened was that his scowl deepened.

"I said get out of here!"

An altercation between some other Skaters and a Scrap boy down the hall distracted Gonzalo. The Scrap boy was on the ground on his back. The Skaters were shouting at the Scrap, accusing him of trying to dye his hair black to look like a Skater. The Scrap boy pleaded that his white hair was only dark because it was dirty.

"Are you deaf, kid?" the bull-horned Skater shouted in Gonzalo's face.

Gonzalo ignored the Skater and rushed toward the Scrap who had been forced into a corner and was getting kicked. Gonzalo wedged himself between the Skaters and the Scrap and held his hand out like a traffic cop, signaling stop. The Skaters were momentarily struck dumb. He could understand how they'd be confused because even he didn't know what the hell he was doing. They were all bigger than him, by a large margin. Even the Scrap on the ground was bigger.

"You think you're gonna stop us?" a Skater in dirty clothes with filth-covered hands said. He walked forward, like he was going to brush Gonzalo off. Gonzalo shoved him. It took all of his strength to force the guy back, but he tried not to let the effort show. He never looked away from the filthy Skater's eyes, and he didn't blink. He slowly nodded his head.

The Skaters were truly confused now. They examined Gonzalo from head to toe, probably wondering whether Gonzalo was some sort of MMA whiz, or had a bottle of hydrochloric acid from the chemistry lab in his back pocket. or if he was flat-out bluffing, which he was. The Scrap boy bolted away, and Gonzalo got a fist in the mouth at the same time. He stumbled with the blow, but managed to stay on his feet, and ran.

The Skaters chased. With each heaving breath, red spit blew from Gonzalo's split lip. The Skaters' gleeful laughter grew louder behind him. At a junction with another hall, the Scrap boy went left, and Gonzalo went right. The hallway ahead dead-ended. There weren't any staircases ahead, or junctions with other halls. He'd trapped himself. Gonzalo skidded to a stop at the next classroom and found the door open. He ran inside and slammed the door shut behind him. He grabbed the nearest classroom chair and wedged the back of the chair under the door's handle. It was a good trick, but it wouldn't work forever.

The door handle swiveled. The door opened half-an-inch, but the chair wedge stopped it.

BOOM. The door rattled from the impact. They were going to get in. He scanned the empty classroom for a weapon. A shard of glass. A hunk of cinderblock. Hell, he'd take a ruler at this point. There was nothing but four other chairs, gray plates of steel where the windows should have been, and a white projector screen spread out on the crud-covered floor like a picnic blanket with ghosts of dingy shoe prints across it.

BOOM. One of the metal legs of the wedged chair bent with the impact. This was gonna be bad. The effort they were putting into bashing this door down meant they weren't gonna let him go. They were going to hurt him. He tried to make his hands into fists, but he couldn't stop them from shaking.

BOOM! The wood of the door splintered.

"Hey," he heard a voice whisper.

Gonzalo looked around the room like he was losing his mind. He swore he'd just heard a voice. And then he saw her. The Slut girl who'd stared at him in the quad, except her hair was blue now, and she'd painted black all around her eyes so that they looked like empty sockets. She was leaning out of an air vent in the wall. She held herself in the push-up position with her hands on the floor. Her forearms were dirty, but her lipstick was hot pink and glossy. Her crop top hung down, her olive skin was glazed in sweat, and she held his stare. This had to be some sort of mirage.

BOOM! He heard the wood of the door crack. The Skaters were about to get in.

"Quick, come with me," she said and pushed herself backwards into the air duct with surprising speed.

The dark hole beckoned. The vent cover hung down below it. Gonzalo ran and dove into the wall. His skin slid across the metal floor of the dark duct and it hurt, but he'd made it all the way inside.

"Pull the string!" she whispered from the dark.

Gonzalo looked down and saw a white string running along next to him on the floor of the vent. He grasped it and pulled it taut. He saw that the string ran through an O-ring screw at the opening of the vent. Pulling the string lifted the air vent grille cover back up into place, like it had never been dislodged at all.

The next BOOM was more of a CRASH, although muffled, and he heard the Skaters rush into the classroom. Then it got quiet. After a minute he heard them leave. They started joking around about something else as their voices faded. The metal walls all around Gonzalo were cool to the touch. The sound of the school was muted and distant.

A flame sparked to life right in front of his face. Its light illuminated the area around them. The Slut who was now dressed like a Freak, who had just saved his ass, was right in front of him, holding a lighter. Their faces were inches apart, separated by a steady flame.

"Why'd you help me?" Gonzalo blurted out.

Her jaw dropped and her mouth stretched into an O. "You talked," she said.

"So?" Gonzalo said. He tried to sound incredulous, but he was shocked too.

"I didn't know you could."

"You didn't answer my question."

"They were going to kill you."

"I probably could have handled them."

She burst out in laughter, at a whisper's volume.

"They were chasing me 'cause I'd already kicked their ass last week," Gonzalo said. "They wanted a rematch."

She only whisper-laughed harder. Her teeth twinkled in the light of the butane flame.

"They were after you 'cause you helped that Scrap," she said. Her laughter trickled away, but her smile remained.

"Have you been watching me?"

She broke eye contact. "Just that thing now in the hall."

She was bad at lying, and it was kind of cute. Her face got hyper-serious, like a soap opera actress. He wondered if she'd been watching him from the vents for a long time.

"So what's with the hair? Are you in one gang or two?" he said.

"Something like that."

"Do you think you could get me in? You guys have food, right?"

He was trying to sound practical about it, but the truth was he was ready to follow this girl into a gas chamber. It felt so good to be talking to someone again, and to finally be around someone he actually felt he could trust. He was also dying to gently mess up her lipstick.

She started inching backwards, away from him.

"Trust me, it's not for you," she said.

"What does that mean?"

"You're a good guy, Gonzalo."

"Wait, don't leave."

She retreated from him faster, the glow of her lighter going with her.

"Don't follow me," she said, before the little flame by her face winked out.

He followed anyway.